What do I do?

Oriel couldn't imagine how much more difficult this would be if Vijay or someone else were pushing her around, telling her what to do.

"If I'm pregnant, I'm keeping the baby." Her eyes grew damp. It felt good to acknowledge that, even though it turned her crystal clear future into a blurred vision through a fogged glass.

He nodded thoughtfully, while his eyes narrowed with intensity.

"And if you're pregnant...it's definitely mine."

The way he said it made her heart lurch unsteadily in her chest. She wanted to set her chin with indignation, but it didn't sound as though he was questioning her. At the same time, she realized this was her chance to firmly eject him from her life if she wanted to.

She couldn't.

She swallowed the hot constriction in her throat. "Today I learned that everything I thought I knew about my birth parents was a lie. I wouldn't do that to my own child. You are definitely the father."

"Then, if you're pregnant," he spoke with steady resolve, "I'll propose."

The Secret Sisters

When their paths cross, expect explosions!

World-renowned model Oriel Cuvier and esteemed fashion designer Nina Menendez are complete strangers. But unbeknownst to them, they share a shocking secret that, once revealed, will shake their worlds to their core!

And the similarities don't end there because everything is set to get even more complicated with the arrival of two commanding men who set their hearts racing and their skin on fire! Will they both succumb to the temptation…?

Read Oriel's story in
Married for One Reason Only
Available now!

And look out for Nina's story
Manhattan's Most Scandalous Reunion
Coming soon!

Escape into the scandalous world of Dani Collins's sexy and irresistible duet The Secret Sisters.

Dani Collins

MARRIED FOR ONE REASON ONLY

HARLEQUIN
PRESENTS

HARLEQUIN®

PRESENTS®

PLEASE RECYCLE
THIS PRODUCT IS RECYCLABLE

Recycling programs
for this product may
not exist in your area.

ISBN-13: 978-1-335-56786-4

Married for One Reason Only

Copyright © 2021 by Dani Collins

This edition published by arrangement with Harlequin Books S.A.

For questions and comments about the quality of this book, please contact us at CustomerService@Harlequin.com.

Harlequin Enterprises ULC
22 Adelaide St. West, 40th Floor
Toronto, Ontario M5H 4E3, Canada
www.Harlequin.com

Printed in U.S.A.

Canadian **Dani Collins** knew in high school that she wanted to write romance for a living. Twenty-five years later, after marrying her high school sweetheart, having two kids with him, working at several generic office jobs and submitting countless manuscripts, she got The Call. Her first Harlequin novel won the Reviewers' Choice Award for Best First in Series from *RT Book Reviews*. She now works in her own office, writing romance.

Books by Dani Collins

Harlequin Presents

Cinderella's Royal Seduction
A Hidden Heir to Redeem Him
Confessions of an Italian Marriage
Innocent in the Sheikh's Palace
What the Greek's Wife Needs
Her Impossible Baby Bombshell

Once Upon a Temptation

Beauty and Her One-Night Baby

Secret Heirs of Billionaires

The Maid's Spanish Secret

Signed, Sealed...Seduced

Ways to Ruin a Royal Reputation

Visit the Author Profile page at Harlequin.com for more titles.

In this trying time, I'm so grateful I've been able to continue writing stories that lift my own spirits and hopefully lift yours. I couldn't have done it without the wonderful teams at Harlequin and Mills & Boon, particularly my editor, Megan Haslam. My heartfelt thanks goes out to all of them for their support and dedication to delivering hope and happiness to readers everywhere.

CHAPTER ONE

ORIEL CUVIER OPENED her hotel room door anticipating birthday roses and confronted a cleaning gent with a mop.

Mon Dieu, even the maintenance men were exceedingly attractive in Italy. Her startled gaze had gone straight to the yellow bucket, but as she dragged her attention upward, she arrived at eyes that were so dark they were nearly black. Much like the cup of espresso had awakened her senses an hour ago, she felt as though she was yanked from dull, mundane thoughts to a readiness to experience everything her day had to offer.

"*Mi scusi.* I heard you were out." His Italian was stilted, his smile a tense, flat stretch of his lips that apologized for his butchering of the language. "I was told to clean a wet." His voice was as deeply seductive as Italians were purported to be while his accent and dark coloring suggested he was South Asian.

Oriel had always felt an inexplicable kinship with people from that corner of the world, even though her parentage was supposedly a mixed couple from Eastern Europe.

"En Français?" she suggested. "Or English?"

"English. Thank you." His speech became as crisp and flawless as a graduate from a British boarding school. "I was told you were out for the day and I should clean a spill."

Honestly, he could be employed in her line of work with those sharp cheekbones, sensual mouth, mussed high-top haircut and devil-may-care stubble. He was substantially taller than her five-eleven, and his broad shoulders strained the seams on his blue boiler suit.

"I didn't request anyone," she said in bemusement.

"Who is it?" Her agent, Payton, spoke in her ear.

"Oh, one minute." She had forgotten her call and pointed at her wireless earbud so the hotel worker would know she wasn't speaking to him. "There's a man at the door, but there seems to be a mistake. I didn't call anyone."

"The maid texted me." The cleaner brought his phone from his deep pocket.

"The maids haven't been in yet," she said.

How was this godlike, educated man pushing a string mop? With that build, he could be laying bricks or bouncing clubs at the very least—which would also be a complete waste of a startlingly magnificent presence. The camera would love him.

She loved him. Oriel saw beautiful men all day every day, but none had ever emanated this sort of powerful energy that almost had her taking a step back in awe while wanting to bask in his presence at the same time. It was like an electric current that made her nerve endings tingle.

And even though handsome men rarely affected her, she had a nearly unbearable urge to twirl her hair and cock her head and wait breathlessly for him to speak.

"Send him away," Payton said in her ear.

She probably should have. Her career was her entire focus these days, providing the sense of achievement that otherwise eluded her. She would never admit to anyone the profound sense of inadequacy that stalked her, or that she had a hole inside her that craved approval and attention. It didn't even make sense. She had everything anyone could want—health, wealth, intelligence, and independence along with looks that ticked all the boxes for modern ideals of beauty.

She would be mocked to death if she revealed her feeling of being "less than," so she pushed her angst into climbing toward the very top of her field, allowing nothing to distract her, including men.

Suddenly she had nothing but time for watching how this stranger swiped his thumb across a screen, though. He studied it with an air of concentration. The strength of her fascination was embarrassing, but she couldn't help it.

He flicked his gaze up to meet hers, catching her giving him moon eyes like a love-struck adolescent.

It caused a swoop in her stomach as though she'd crested a wave.

"My mistake. Wrong floor. And my colleague has dealt with the issue." He pocketed the phone while his penetrating stare kept hold of hers.

Her skin tightened and her bones grew soft. She knew when a man was interested in her. She rarely reciprocated such things, but here she stood. Involuntarily reciprocating with every fiber of her being.

It was disconcerting to be so overcome. To feel so helpless to do anything but stand there while he took in her snug, high-waisted corduroy trousers with matching suspenders over a low-cut floral top.

His mouth relaxed, and the angle of his shoulders eased. It wasn't all sexual interest, though. There was something else in his study. Not calculation, precisely. Investigation? He liked what he saw, but he was delving into her eyes as though looking for answers to unasked questions.

She wasn't sure what that cooler side of his appraisal was about, but it was far more unsettling than if he'd worn a wolfish grin and said something suggestive. She could have handled that with flirt or frost. Whatever *this* was made her neck prickle with premonition. This man was going to change her life.

How silly, she scolded herself, trying to pretend she wasn't flushing with her reaction. But she was filled with anticipation and something else—her own curiosity. A far-reaching sense of possibility. Excitement.

"Was there anything else I could do for you while I'm here?" he asked in a bland tone.

The tension left the air with a withering dissipation.

She was reading him wrong, she realized with chagrin. He was an employee of the hotel waiting for her to dismiss him. That's all the lengthy, charged silence had been about. Could he tell she was drooling over him, wanting him to feel the same way she did? How mortifying.

"Yes, actually." As a hot, self-conscious blush stung her cheeks, she latched on to the first excuse she could think of to cover why she had kept him lingering. "The ceiling fan in my bedroom is rattling." It had driven her crazy all night. "I haven't had time to report it. I wondered if that was something you could fix?"

In the pause, she could have sworn she heard the gears in his head give a whir of computation. Then, "I can have a look."

Oriel's heart was pounding with nerves, but she pressed her back to the wall, allowing him to enter the small passageway.

He left the mop and bucket outside the door and briefly crowded her, seeming to steal all the oxygen from this tiny foyer.

Her instincts prickled another warning, not because she thought he posed a physical danger, but from awareness of the power that radiated from him. He could seduce her without even trying. Her blood was turning to molasses in the seconds that he loomed close and allowed one corner of his mouth to dent. Those dark eyes of his promised long, sensual nights.

She had never felt this way on meeting a man. It was pure magic, holding his gaze and feeling connected at a level that went far beyond what happened between strangers.

Then his expression hardened with refusal. He snapped his gaze forward and stepped into the room.

He knows. And had decided he didn't want to make a play for her.

Her whole body went into free fall, and her self-worth crumpled on impact. Oriel felt rejection *very* deeply. She had her theories as to why—being adopted and an only child. In her observations, people who had spats with siblings and were still loved afterward had more resilience to the small scuffs of life.

She hated that she allowed small rebuffs to strike such a deep place inside her, but they always did. The tiniest slights landed directly on that achingly tender center of her soul.

It was such a perverse reaction, because coming on to a guest could cost this man his job. She had no room in her life for romance, anyway. What did she care if a man she would never see again thought she was worth his time or not?

Nevertheless, she was so stung she thought about asking him to come back later, but he was already trying the switch on the wall and looking at the fan over the coffee table. He wasn't wearing a ring and didn't have a tan line where one was missing, she noted. She was annoyed with herself for looking.

"The one in the bedroom," she murmured, waving across the small lounge.

"You didn't let him in." Payton's voice startled her again.

She seriously had to get her head on straight. "I did. It's fine."

"This is how scandals are created!"

"With me doing what? I live like a nun." She did more scandalous things in public, parading down runways in her underwear, than she did in private. She didn't travel with any jewelry worth stealing or have any secret predilections worth exposing, either.

She lowered onto the sofa, deliberately turning her back on the man flipping the switch inside her bedroom door. Trying not to think about how his shoes had looked far pricier than the kind she expected a man in his profession to be able to afford.

Perhaps they'd been left by a guest and happened to fit him. She occasionally left wine or clothing behind when she traveled. Most hotels had an arrangement in which the housekeeping staff could divvy up abandoned items as a small job perk.

"If someone saw you letting him in, it could ruin the interest from Duke Rhodes," Payton said.

Ugh. Right. The reason for his call. Oriel had been introduced to the aging action star at a cocktail party a few nights ago.

"Do you really think I should go to Cannes with him? He's twice my age."

"He likes you."

"We spoke for five minutes." He had tried to kiss her on the lips. "I honestly couldn't say whether I liked him or not." She hadn't. "Have *you* spoken to him? Caught a whiff of his breath?" she added with a wince of recollection.

"It's part of his image that he always has a cigarette in his hand."

"And a drink in the other? He smelled like scotch." The sour, lingering stench of heavy drinking had emanated from his pores.

"It's *good* scotch, angel. He smashes box offices. The cameras follow him everywhere. Do you want to take your career to the next level or not?"

"Of course, but that's my only week of vacation this year." And her parents were celebrating their thirtieth anniversary. "It will chop into the first two days of it."

"You can fly straight from Cannes to Tours. His people will pay for all of it."

Payton was the best in the business. One didn't move from runway to international ad campaigns without a man like him paving the way. Thanks to him, she no longer shared a room with other models and was given first-class suites like this one, with gorgeous views of the Milan skyline.

Even so, she found his strategy disheartening. What about working hard? What about advancing on merit? Why resort to timeworn gimmicks? Who would respect her if she couldn't respect herself?

"I'm concerned about what a man like Duke Rhodes would expect if—"

A dull thump and a sharp curse had her sitting up and twisting to see into the bedroom.

The maintenance man had draped a spare blanket over the bed and was flat in the middle of it, pushing the fan off his chest while blood welled on his forehead.

"I have to go." She pulled out her earbuds and leaped to her feet.

"Be careful. Stay on the bed," Oriel Cuvier rushed in to say. "I'll call down for help."

Vijay Sahir sat up to set the contraption on the floor. "I'm fine."

He was rattled and bruised, but it was his own fault. He'd been scanning the room for clues about her, eavesdropping on her conversation while thinking less than honorable thoughts about her and the bed he was standing on.

He'd been paying no attention to the fan he'd been pretending to fix, giving the housing an absent wiggle. The damned thing had come down on top of him, ringing his bell hard enough to leave him angry with himself for being so careless.

"That could have come down on *me* last night." She eyed the wires dangling from the ceiling. "Your head is bleeding. You need first aid, and I need to make a proper complaint."

She stepped around the broken fan and reached for the cordless phone in its bedside charger.

"No!" He threw himself across the bed to catch her wrist. "They'll fire me."

They wouldn't. Couldn't. He didn't work here. Which would be even trickier to explain.

"Well…" Even wearing a frown of consternation, she was the most beautiful woman he'd ever seen.

Her profile said she was of mixed Romanian and Turkish blood, adopted at birth by a French couple. Vijay would be damned if she didn't look Indian with that natural golden tone in her skin and those strong brows. Hell, in person she looked even more like Bollywood legend Lakshmi Dalal with her big brown eyes, her delicate bone structure in an oval face, her near-black hair in an untamed disarray of wavy curls. Her mouth was naked, but still made a bold, full-lipped statement when she pursed it stubbornly.

"I won't let them fire you." She stood tall and wore the confidence of wealth.

Don't be a hypocrite, Vijay. You're wealthy, too.

Even more so very soon, but he had a well-earned aversion to spoiled heiresses.

"I'm still new here." Whether she took that as new to this hotel or this country didn't matter. Both were very weak versions of the truth. He unconsciously stroked his thumb against her incredibly soft skin in persuasion.

Her breath caught, and a confused spark flashed into her eyes, one that arced across to stab an answering heat into the pit of his belly.

Everything about her was slicing his brain into

sections, making it difficult to remember she was the subject of an inquiry. Or possibly an innocent bystander chosen for her resemblance to a Bollywood icon. Either way, she was the key to ensuring Vijay's sister wasn't conned out of her fortune.

Vijay made himself release Oriel's wrist and rolled to his feet on the far side of the bed. "If you give me an hour, I'll have all of this sorted," he promised. "I need to fetch a few tools."

He wasn't a certified electrician, but he could rewire a fan.

"I actually have an appointment." She glanced at the clock.

"I can let myself in." That's what he'd been planning to do with his ill-gotten, all-access housekeeping card. He had taken a chance, hoping she would already be out for the day. The mop had been a prop, the knock a precaution.

"I suppose." Her doubtful gaze dropped to the name tag on his borrowed coveralls, then came back to his eyebrow. "You're still bleeding. Did you realize that? Please sit down." She nodded at the edge of the bed and disappeared into the bathroom.

He touched the wet trickle that was winding its way down his temple. When he saw the blood, he swiped the sleeve of the coveralls across it, leaving a dark streak on the heavy blue cotton.

"I'll survive. Don't worry about it," he called.

"No, let me." She came back with a small bag marked with a red cross. "I asked you to fix the fan. This is my fault."

He hesitated, then sat on the bed and closed his eyes, trying not to picture the way the suspenders framed her breasts and cleavage so enticingly. He briefly thought about coming clean and saying, *Look, I need your DNA*.

A container ship of worms would open at that point, and for what? The chance that Oriel was related to Lakshmi Dalal was near zero. As far as Vijay could discern, a con man was leaping on Oriel's resemblance to Lakshmi to get his hands on the money Vijay and his sister would make as they merged ViKay Security Solutions with a bigger, global enterprise.

On the very slim chance that their "client" was telling the truth and Lakshmi did have a lost child out there, Vijay owed the man his utmost discretion. The mystery seemed too coincidental to be believed, though. When Vijay had booked this trip to Europe, he had seen an opportunity to get to the bottom of things. He'd tacked on this side trip to Milan so he could intercept Oriel. All he had to do was pretend to be a hotel worker for another few minutes, steal her toothbrush, and get on with his life.

There was a tearing sound, the pungent scent of alcohol, then a cool swipe on his brow that left a sting in its wake.

He couldn't help his small wince.

"Sorry." She blew on it, making his eyes snap open.

Her blouse gaped, and he was staring straight down the shadowed valley between her lace-cupped breasts. Lovely, abundant breasts that his palms itched to gather and massage.

He deliberately set his hands onto the blankets next to his hips, but he could still smell the fragrance of tropical body wash clinging to her skin and wanted to rub his face into her throat. He wanted to keep going, dislodging the edges of her shirt so he could find her nipples—

"There." She set a bandage over the cut, cupped his face in her cool hands, and *kissed* the injury.

He was so shocked, he snapped his head back.

"I'm sorry." Her hands fell away, but she was frozen, still leaning over him, as shocked as he was. "I didn't mean to—I have a little cousin who—Obviously, you're not a child. I'm so embar—"

"Do it again." The words shouldn't have left his chest, but there they were, rumbling up into the space between their lips. He didn't lower his attention back to her breasts. He kept his face tilted up and his gaze on her mouth.

For endless seconds, they were held in that state while she made up her mind. Then slowly, slowly she lowered her head. Her mouth pressed to his, delicate as a butterfly landing on a rose. He lost his sight. Impressions came to him in flashes as her lips slid against his—the softness of flower petals and the crushed scent of them filling his head. Velvety heat in her breath and the dark, sweetly sensual flavor of her as they both opened their mouths wider to deepen the kiss.

He skimmed his touch along her forearms, catching lightly at her elbows, inviting her closer. She braced her hands on his shoulders and leaned against him, slanted her head and sank into their kiss, stealing every thought in his head.

It was the most frustratingly delectable kiss of his life. He wanted to drag her in and take control, but he was too enthralled by letting her have her way. She sipped and experimented and decided what she liked before she pressed deeper. Tasted him more boldly.

He groaned and signaled more firmly on her arms, urging her to be more aggressive.

Her knees dug into the mattress on either side of his hips. The warm weight of her settled on his thighs. Gratification rumbled in his throat. He swept his palms to her shoulders and roamed his touch over the warmth of her body through silk. He followed the straps of the suspenders, enjoying the lithe flex of her back and the furrowed texture of her trousers where he made circles on the flare of her hips.

She sighed and inched her knees on the mattress, settling more deeply into his lap. She switched the slant of her head to the other side with barely a breath for either of them.

This boiler suit was a size too small. It pulled tautly across his back and shoulders and against his knees as he splayed his legs and looped his arms around her, trying to drag her even tighter into his lap. Her hair tangled in his fingers as he cupped the back of her head and gave in to the craving taking over him. He swept his tongue into her mouth and sucked on her lips, wanting to absorb her into himself.

She made a noise that was a helpless pang of pleasure, pure seduction, and shivered. Her arms folded behind his neck and she pressed even closer, so all he could think was how badly he wanted the heat of her sex scorching where he had hardened to titanium.

His hands cupped under her bottom and, purely on instinct, his arms hardened around her. He rolled, setting her beneath him on the bed. Now he could kiss her throat the way he'd been dying to, tasting the small hollow at the base. Her hands went into his hair and—

"Mon Dieu. Stop."

He lifted his head. Her horrified gaze was pinned to the ceiling. When she met his own, she pressed her head more deeply into the mattress, expression appalled.

Bloody hell. He wasn't a hotel employee, which would be bad enough. He had lied his way in here.

Vijay pushed himself off her, feeling as though he left a layer of his skin adhered to her. It *hurt*. He didn't dare look down to see whether these damned coveralls were disguising his arousal.

She was sitting up and smoothing her hair, ensuring her blouse buttons were secure. "That shouldn't have happened."

"No," he agreed. "It shouldn't. I'll leave." He did.

CHAPTER TWO

IT WAS A good thing Oriel's appointment this morning had only been a fitting. The main requirement of her had been to stand still and be quiet. She would have been useless at anything else. Her mind had been completely occupied by the most salacious kiss of her life.

Apparently, she harbored fantasies of making love to strange men who appeared at the door like the mythical pizza delivery hookup. What else could explain the way she'd crawled into his lap and practically offered herself? If she hadn't blinked open her eyes to see the bare wires in the ceiling, and been reminded where she was and that he was a complete stranger, she might have gone all the way with him!

Maybe it had been a dream, she tried telling herself as she looked around. The fan was back in place, the spare blanket gone, the bed made and the pillows fluffed. The suite wore the tidy polish of an efficient housekeeping visit.

When she tried the switch, the fan was perfectly silent, not rattling the way it had last night.

Should she call down and leave a message to thank him? Leave a tip with a note? What would she say? *You left* me *rattled. Can you fix* that?

The part that was torturing her most was, why? Why had she lost any sense of decorum? Was she that starved for affection?

She did have yearnings for a serious relationship, but she also knew she had to love herself. She couldn't expect someone else to *make* her feel loved.

Maybe she should start dating herself, she thought, smirking around the mouth of the bottle of water she was drinking. Rather than seek outside validation, she could take herself out for dinner. It was her birthday, after all.

Actually, maybe she would do that, she decided, and started to search for a restaurant to make a reservation. She was distracted by an email from her agent. Payton had sent through a confirmation on her trip to Cannes in May. *Magnifique*, she thought dourly.

Her mother had also left a message about Oriel's gown for the anniversary party. Madame Estelle would be annoyed when Oriel told her she wouldn't arrive until the morning of, thanks to her red carpet appearance with Duke Rhodes.

She bit back a sigh and threw her phone down while she began to change, still irritated by this Cannes idea. She was trying to make her mark without riding her mother's famous coattails, but she would be riding the coattails of a one-time heartthrob who wanted to look as though he could still get off-camera action in the form of a twenty-five-year-old model. Payton would say it was how the game was played, but Oriel felt like a sellout.

She didn't have time to stand around brooding, though. She had a casting call for a luxury eyewear brand in an hour. Such things ran notoriously late, but she was always five minutes early. It was mid-March and the breeze still sharp, but she changed into a filmy summer dress that showed lots of her long, tanned legs.

She moved into the bathroom to brush out her hair and fix her makeup and found a note where her toothbrush ought to have been.

The scrawled handwriting took her a moment to work out.

Apologies. I dropped your toothbrush while washing the dust from my hands. The fan is in order now. Call me if you have further concerns.

There was a phone number in place of a signature.

Hmm. Was he offering his number in a professional capacity or giving her his number?

She tucked the note in her bag while she applied a bold red to her speculative smile, pondering whether she would text him and what she might say.

After a quick check that she had a pair of heels, and a romance novel to read while she waited, she threw on her overcoat and hurried out.

* * *

Vijay ordered a beer while he waited for a table at an upscale restaurant a few blocks from the hotel. When he checked his phone, he saw a text from his sister, Kiran, asking how the merger discussions had gone and why he wasn't home yet. He replied,

Good. I was delayed. Will fly home tomorrow.

He didn't mention that the offer they'd received was so generous, he was more concerned than ever that she was being targeted for her fortune. He also skipped telling her that he'd stolen a toothbrush to prove it.

Vijay had sent the toothbrush overnight to a DNA lab. When he returned to Mumbai, he fully expected their client, Jalil Dalal, to refuse to give up his own sample to determine whether he was Oriel's uncle. Vijay was calling the man's bluff, dismantling the excuse Jalil was using to spend so much time with Kiran.

Jalil had seen Kiran speak in Delhi at a symposium about women in business where she had relayed how she and Vijay had grown their security company from a scrappy start-up to acquisition offers. Jalil had followed her to Mumbai, where he had asked her to help him with a "highly confidential, very personal assignment."

Kiran was beautiful and intelligent and successful enough for any man to want her on her own merit, but Jalil's request was not in their wheelhouse.

Vijay and Kiran had started ViKay Security Solutions to protect themselves after taking a difficult stand that had destroyed the life they'd grown up in. A few years ago, they had accidentally developed a facial recognition system that accounted for skin tone, scars and makeup.

Their system was so accurate, global powerhouse TecSec wanted to acquire it. The owner was prepared to make Vijay the VP of his Asia division, and Kiran would have an executive role overseeing programming and development for the entire organization. They could finally put their past behind them and redeem their reputations.

This was *not* the time to run private investigations searching for imaginary children of deceased Bollywood stars.

That's what Kiran had been asked to do, though. Jalil Dalal had seen a model who resembled his dead sister and claimed Oriel must be his secret niece. Jalil didn't have proof Lakshmi had been pregnant. She had gone to Europe around the time of Oriel's birth and made a few remarks before she died—of a broken heart, according to Jalil—but that was all he knew.

It was the kind of tale that appealed directly to Kiran's soft heart, though. She had swallowed it hook, line and sinker.

Vijay sipped his beer, almost wishing the story was true. It would give him an excuse to see Oriel Cuvier again. He'd been in a state of low-key arousal all day thinking about their kiss. It shouldn't have happened, but he was not nearly as remorseful as he ought to be.

Oriel definitely possessed the same sensual allure as Lakshmi Dalal, he acknowledged sardonically, but it was beyond outlandish that she could be the screen queen's secret child.

For starters, the beloved actress wouldn't have such a scandal in her past. Lakshmi Dalal was India's *didi*, first charming her way into hearts with a portrayal of an older sister who was determined to give her kidney to her ailing younger brother. In a later film, she disguised herself as a young man, both becoming a symbol of feminism to girls and indelibly imprinting herself into adolescent male fantasies when she put on a sari and danced in the rain. From there, she became a mainstay in romantic musicals, a seal of wholesomeness that reassured all parents it was safe to allow their children to watch.

Jalil claimed that's why this had to be handled so delicately. He didn't want his sister's memory tainted, but Jalil lived off what remained of Lakshmi's earnings. That had to be running low by now. He was looking for fresh income, and Kiran was a convenient target.

That might be a cynical view, but Vijay didn't trust anyone except Kiran. And after his failed engagement, he would do anything to protect Kiran from similar disillusionment.

He flicked to the next email and saw his presentation to the hotel had resulted in an agreement in principle to move forward with the security package he had pitched to them.

Vijay was the king of multitasking. He'd detoured here on his way home from the merger meeting, booked himself into Oriel's hotel and wrangled a tour of the security system by pitching his own. That had given him the knowledge to break into a maintenance area undetected. He'd finagled himself a housekeeping card, talked his way into the room of a hotel guest, and retrieved what he needed to expose his sister's paramour as the fraud he was.

A man in his position should behave more honorably, he supposed. By misleading his sister and going behind Oriel's back, he was perpetuating the sorts of lies and betrayals he'd suffered.

As if karma wished to offer him a chance to make better choices, he absently lifted his gaze to the door and watched Oriel walk in. A jolt of electrical thrill went through him.

Dusk was closing in, but she looked as though she'd just left a beach with her hair windswept and her skin glowing. She wore makeup that emphasized her wide eyes and lush mouth. As she stood in the doorway, she unbelted her coat to reveal an airy dress with a ruffle across her chest. He leaned down slightly and caught a glimpse of her slender calves.

He was definitely in the throes of a sexual crush, but she had *climbed into his lap* this morning as though it was where she was meant to belong.

Heiress, his brain reminded him starkly, but his lap twitched with lascivious memory.

He watched her glance around uncertainly. Meeting someone? *Who?* The most intense aggression punched him in the gut, but he already knew that jealousy was a pointless emotion. If the person you were committed to wanted someone else, they were already gone.

Oriel smiled as the maître d' greeted her. She must have been informed the restaurant was full, because her smile fell away. Like him, she seemed to be invited to wait at the bar until a table became free. She sent a considering look his direction, and her eyes widened as she met his gaze.

Don't, he told himself, even as he stepped off his stool and nodded at it, inviting her to join him. Hot tension invaded his belly as he waited for her to decide.

Her dark red lipstick briefly disappeared as she rolled her lips together.

Oh, those lips. So soft. So hungry. How would they feel traveling other places?

With another faltering smile, she pointed and told the maître d' she would join him. She moved like a ballerina as she approached, hair bouncing as she seemed to float on air. Her coat fell open, and her dress seemed to be made of something delicate like gossamer. It clung subtly to her breasts, and he had to exert all his control not to ogle her.

"Hello again." Her cheeks might have stained with color, but it was difficult to tell in this light. "I should apologize for this morning."

"No, I was out of line." Way, way out of line. "It was excellent taste on my part, but poor judgment."

Her mouth twitched with reluctant humor. Her gaze flickered over his collared shirt and tailored pants, then widened with startled comprehension.

"Are you on a date?"

"I had a meeting." He debated how much to tell her. "I pitched my security company. I'm Vijay." He offered his hand, deliberately withholding his surname.

"Oriel." Her wariness dissolved into a bright smile as she put her hand in his. "You didn't sign your note. Did you think I would get you in trouble if I knew your name?"

He practically fell into the dark, sensual pools of her eyes. The soft feel of her hand in his was the only thing keeping him from drowning.

"I'm quite sure you'll get me into trouble." It was supposed to be a joke, but the truth sent a skip through his chest. "Oriel."

She laughed, and of course it was the sparkling kind that was heady as champagne bubbles. "I'll try not to. Vijay."

Spending more time with her was a terrible idea, but as he held her hand, the noise around them dimmed, and all he saw was her. It was like taking a hit of a potent drug.

The bartender broke the spell, asking for her order. Oriel requested white wine and slid onto the stool Vijay had vacated.

"Thank you for fixing my fan. It seems perfect now."

He'd had to sneak around the maid's schedule, but as he subtly drank in her scent, he had no regrets about being inconvenienced.

"You didn't want to eat at the hotel?" Ironically, he had avoided the restaurant there out of concern he would run into her. He set his elbow on the bar, pleased that the crowded space meant he had to stand so close that her knee brushed his thigh.

"It caters to tourists. I wanted to treat myself to something more inspiring. It's my birthday. Are you also celebrating? Did your meeting go well?"

"It did, but I'm just having a beer." He would find somewhere else to eat. This was madness, even talking to her again. "Happy birthday," he said as her wine arrived.

They saluted with their drinks, and her spine softened as she sipped.

"Long day? What do you do?" He already knew, but he liked that she had to lean close to him to be heard over the din.

"Model. I've been at a casting call for hours. They were whittling it down, so I had to keep doing my thing as more higher-ups were called in." She lowered a pair of invisible sunglasses and made an O of her mouth.

He didn't care what the sunglasses looked like. He'd buy them and the car that went with it. "Did you get it?"

"Who knows, but it went well enough that it's

another reason to celebrate. Only one, though." She tilted her glass. "I have an early call for a photo shoot tomorrow. Then I'm on a plane back to New York."

"You live there?"

"Paris, but I spend a lot of time in New York. Actually, I spend a lot of time on airplanes." She sipped again. "You? I assume your maintenance work is a side gig while you get your company off the ground? Why Milan?"

Damn. He had implied that he had moved here.

"It's a temporary thing." He considered how to stick as close to the truth as possible. "We're based in Mumbai, but hoping to expand. I came to Milan because my sister is involved with a man I believe is trying to take advantage of her."

"Oh?" Her expression cooled.

"I can see you judging me." He pointed the mouth of his bottle at her. "Brothers are allowed to be protective, especially when I raised her and she's all I have."

He hadn't meant to reveal that, only to keep her from labeling him as some sort of patriarchal, honor-obsessed throwback.

"You lost your parents?" Her expression softened. "I'm sorry."

"When I was fourteen, yes. She was ten." He drank the last of his beer, trying to rinse away the pall of anguish, old and more recent, that their deaths still left in his throat. "Our grandmother lived with us, but she was quite frail and passed a year later."

"That must have been a very difficult time." Her

brow wrinkled with compassion. "No wonder you're so close and protective of her. Does your sister live here?"

"Mumbai. What about you?" He quickly flipped it so he wouldn't have to dissemble any more than he already had. "Do you have siblings?" Everything online said she was an only child, but he might as well have it straight from her.

"No. I always wished for a brother or sister, but my mother—" She hesitated. "Maman is very wrapped up in her career. She has every right to be. She's a famous soprano. Estelle Fabron?"

He shrugged, feigning unfamiliarity with the name. He only knew it from the mention in Oriel's profile anyway.

"Madame Estelle is beloved in the opera world. Especially here." She kept leaning in to speak against his ear. Her breath tickled, and he was damned close to turning his head and capturing her mouth with his own. "She casts a *long* shadow. It's refreshing to speak to someone who has never heard of her."

Her lips were right there, ripe and tempting. He looked into her eyes, and she was staring at his mouth. *Are we doing this, my beautiful goddess?*

The hostess appeared to say their table was ready. He was not ready to let her go, but his beer was finished.

"Join me," Oriel invited.

It was the moment when Vijay should have insisted he was only here for the one drink, but he couldn't make himself say good-night. Once he used the DNA test to vanquish Jalil, he would continue his life as programmed. It was highly unlikely he would ever see Oriel again. Surely there was no harm in buying her dinner and spending another hour in her company?

Now he was lying to himself as well as her. Or at least feeding himself weak rationalizations, but he waved her to follow the hostess and held Oriel's chair before he took the one opposite.

Oriel opened her menu, but glanced over it at him. "I'd like to buy you dinner. As I said, I'm celebrating, and you did suffer that injury from fixing my fan."

Her glance touched the nick above his brow, which was visible because he'd removed the bandage as soon as it stopped bleeding.

When her gaze dropped to the menu, she bit her lips again.

The prices were on the high side even for Italy. It struck him that she thought he might struggle to afford one meal, let alone two.

Wasn't this an awkward position to be in? Very few women he dined with had ever paid for themselves, let alone bought him a meal. Irrationally, he was insulted by her offer. There was a snobbery to the move that got under his skin—which was his personal baggage coming around on the carousel. He doubted she was *trying* to offend him.

"If one of us pays for the other, it makes this a date," he pointed out. "If this *was* a date, especially our first date, *I* would pay. Yes," he replied in answer to the way her brows lifted. "I'm that sort of man."

Her mouth pursed to hide a smile. "Split it down the middle then? Since we're sharing a table out of convenience? How do you feel about sharing dishes?"

"Depends what you like."

"I like everything." The look she sent him had to be from her stock of smoldering expressions for a camera. Even so, it went into him like a spear, straight to the tightening flesh between his thighs.

He was definitely paying for dinner.

Once they ordered, he said, "You seem to be traveling alone, but I should have asked. Is there anyone you usually dine with?" He had overheard her conversation about appearing with that action star. It had sounded like an innocuous photo op, and his research said she was single.

"I travel too much to date seriously. You?" She subtly braced herself.

"I would not have allowed you to kiss this mouth if it belonged to someone else. Yes," he said as her jaw went slack. "I'm also *that* sort of man." Blunt. Possessive in a reciprocal way. He offered monogamy because he expected it.

Her chin came up. "Did *I* kiss *you*?"

"You absolutely did."

"I didn't hear you objecting. Perhaps speak more clearly next time."

"Will there be a next time? I'm delighted to hear it."

She hid her smile with her wineglass, indignant

but also amused. "Do all the hotel guests receive such personal treatment?"

"Definitely not. You're an exception."

"Hmm." She relaxed and recrossed her legs, bumping his shin beneath the table.

He reflexively caught her ankle between his calves, just long enough to have her startled gaze flash into his so he could watch that haze of sensual awareness come into it.

He released her as quickly as he'd caught her, leaving Oriel breathless.

She didn't believe in fate or destiny, but she was astonished to have bumped into him this way. She had glanced at the menu on the way to her audition, but hadn't had time to make a reservation. For a moment after she arrived, she had thought she would have to settle for room service after all.

Now she was enjoying an Indian-Italian fusion of tandoori duck, curried gnocchi, and tikka masala ravioli with a man she'd been thinking about all day.

He was an intriguing man. Educated and confident and quick-witted, but difficult to read. She wanted to ask him more about how he had come to be working at the hotel, but it sounded as though he was only doing it to make ends meet while he pursued bigger things, maybe paying for his expenses while he was here.

"Tell me about your security business," she invited.

"Most of the credit goes to my sister. She wrote

specialty software, and I matched it to the right components. We literally began with one customer at a time, tailoring it to each client's needs. It's grown to the point that we're close to partnering with a bigger company. Those talks are highly confidential, so I can't say more."

"Sounds like a big break. Good luck. I hope it goes well."

"Thanks. How did you get into modeling? What was your big break?"

"Nepotism," she said wryly. "My mother hoped I would have more vocal talent, but she's a once-in-a-generation unicorn, and I'm adopted, so..."

His brows went up. Most people reacted with curiosity when she offered that information.

"It's public knowledge." She brushed away having revealed such a personal detail. "Maman's career was taking off. She didn't want to interrupt it with a pregnancy, but they wanted a family. Adoption was their perfect solution."

Perhaps *perfect* wasn't the best word. They had approached parenting wholeheartedly, but babies were demanding, and they never found the right time to adopt a second one. They claimed to be fulfilled by the single daughter they had, but Oriel had a twisted, illogical sense that if she'd been different, more winsome maybe, they would have wanted another.

"While I was growing up, Maman hired teachers for me in every type of classical instruction, but I was no prodigy. The closest I came was being scouted for a pop band."

"That suggests you have musical talent." He was looking at her the way he had when he'd stood outside her hotel room door. Penetrating. Collecting hidden data. "Have you tried acting?"

It was nice to have a man look beyond her face and want to know more about *her*, but this level of attention was disconcerting. She wasn't sure why.

"I can do many things reasonably well—dancing and singing and playing piano. I don't have Maman's level of talent, though, so I couldn't bring myself to go into performance arts. I would always be compared to her. Papa is an academic, very intelligent, but I'll never win prizes for literature or physics. I thought I was destined for mediocrity, but the summer I turned fifteen, one of Maman's costume designers asked if I wanted to model some of his designs at his show. It was the first thing I'd found where the bar wasn't already set impossibly high by someone in my family. With modeling, I've been able to grow into my own version of success."

That sense of carving out her own space and rising through the ranks soothed the part of her that struggled to feel good enough. She knew her angst stemmed from her adoption, and it wasn't entirely fair of her to harbor that sense of rejection. From what she knew of her birth mother, the young woman had been in a very difficult position. She'd had an affair with a married man of a different race and didn't feel she could keep the baby that resulted, not without losing all the other pieces of her life.

Oriel didn't resent her for giving her up. Her birth mother had chosen carefully, and Oriel lived an extremely privileged life, but it didn't seem to matter how often she reminded herself of that. She still suffered this bereft sense of having been cast off simply because she was mixed race.

They went on to talk about things. As they finished dessert, she asked the server to split the bill, but Vijay had taken care of it while she had visited the powder room.

"I thought—"

"It's your birthday," he said dismissively. "And you barely ate."

Oriel ran miles every day to keep her figure trim, largely because she had a healthy appetite. Even so, "That was a lot of carbs for a woman who is going to be in a bikini tomorrow."

"You'll be fine," he assured her with smoky admiration.

The potency of this man! She sold seduction for a living and had never experienced anything like his ability to make her swoon with a softly spoken word or a half-lidded glance.

"I...um—" *Control yourself, Oriel.* "I wouldn't have been able to sample all of these dishes if I'd dined alone, so thank you. This was a nice surprise." Beneath the table, she was aware of the toe of her shoe resting next to his. "I guess this is a date now?"

"I guess it is." His smile was only a tiny bit smug.

They finished their drinks and made their way outside.

"Do you dare be seen walking me to the hotel?" she asked.

"I dare anything." His mouth twisted with irony.

"Oh, you're *that* sort of man," she teased.

"And this." He offered his crooked elbow.

She tucked her hand through it as they ambled the few blocks that were bustling with tourists heading out to dine or enjoy the theater.

As they passed a recessed stoop, Oriel spun herself into it, tugging him in with her.

"Would you like to know what sort of woman I am?"

"If you tell me you're the sort who makes love in public, I may have to adjust what kind of man I am." He set his forearms on the door on either side of her head, caging her into the shadowed space created by his wide shoulders.

"Ha. Sorry to disappoint. I'm only the kind who doesn't like that awkward moment wondering if a man will kiss her. I'd rather make it happen. If it's going to."

"I noticed that about you already." He let the tip of his nose playfully brush hers.

"Are you still banging on about how I took advantage of you?" She let her hands rest on his rib cage. "Cry for help. See if someone will rescue you."

"Help," he said faintly, flashing his teeth. "I'm helpless to resist this woman." His lips touched a corner of hers.

She shivered and slid her hands to the backs of his shoulders. She tried to chase his lips, but he switched to kissing the other side of her mouth.

"I don't usually kiss strangers," she whispered.

"Nor I."

"You don't feel like a stranger, though," she admitted, perplexed by how true that was. "It feels like we're..." *Lovers.*

That's what she was thinking. Maybe she said it aloud, because he groaned and covered her mouth with his.

She had been waiting throughout their meal for him to kiss her again. Waiting and waiting.

She sighed with relief and stroked her touch across the landscape of his back, encouraging him to press her into the door, delighting in the way he devastated her with his kiss.

Had she thought she was in control this morning? He had been toying with her, letting her think so. This man knew how to ravage in the most tender way possible, claiming and plundering and pulling her very soul from her body.

At the same time, he gave. Oh, he generously venerated her mouth, silently telling her she was the most precious thing he'd ever tasted. The most exquisite.

Their lips made soft, wet noises while an ache panged in her throat. A sob of surrender. She softened under the press of his heavy body, wanting his weight. Wanting his hard, flat chest compressing her swollen breasts. She wanted to feel his steely thighs naked against hers, bracing hers open. She wanted the unforgiving ridge that was bulging behind his fly to fill her…

"Vijay…" Her hands went down his back, urging him to press into her mound. "Come to my room."

With the same attitude of superhuman strength he'd exhibited this morning, he dragged his head up and sucked in a breath. He straightened so he wasn't touching her at all.

"You have an early morning," he recalled with a ragged edge to his otherwise stern voice. "We should end this here." He looked away into the street.

"Should? Or is that what you want?" she asked through a tight throat.

He muttered something under his breath. "Believe me, Oriel. I want to come to your room. But it's not a good idea."

"Why not?" She hooked her finger in the waistband of his jeans to keep him from retreating further. "We're single. I don't know when I would have another evening free like this."

"And it's your birthday?" He spoke lightly, but there was a note of cynicism in his tone that made her drop her hand away from his jeans.

"What is that supposed to mean?"

"Nothing." He caught her hand. "Except you're flying to New York tomorrow. I won't be here by the time you come back. I have my own work commitments." His thumb stroked across the back of her knuckles. "I don't have one-night stands. I don't think you do, either."

"That's not what this would be, though, would it? I mean, you're right. I'm married to my career right now, but this isn't a hookup. It's... I've met someone I really like. I want to hang on to what little time we have together."

He swore again and gathered her up, swooping his mouth down to crash across hers. She tasted the conflict in him and poured herself into the kiss, enticing. Pleading, maybe.

When he lifted his head, they were both panting. His heart was pounding so hard in his chest, her fingertips felt as though they bounced where they rested on his pec.

She started to take his hand and lead him back onto the sidewalk, but hesitated.

"Would it be bad for you to be seen going into a room? I'll walk through the lobby and you can use the service elevator. You have a card, don't you? You don't have to knock when you come to my room."

His arms hardened to keep her in the shadowed stoop with him. "I'll knock. If you change your mind, no hard feelings."

"I won't change my mind." She slid her arms around him long enough to kiss under his chin. "But you're right. I never do this. I don't have anything. Protection, I mean. Can you?"

His breath left him in a jagged gust. "Yes. I'll take care of it."

"Thank you. I'll see you soon."

CHAPTER THREE

DON'T GO, VIJAY told himself.

That advice might have been easier to obey if he hadn't been staying in the same damned hotel. If he hadn't had to pass her floor to get to his own.

I want to hang on to what little time we have together.

Him too, for more reasons than the fact he was randy as hell after hours of flirting and footsie, then a kiss that had set his blood alight. He *liked* her. Enough that he felt like a heel for keeping secrets from her.

She wasn't looking for a relationship, though. Many things about their lives would remain a mystery from each other. Some people made this sort of relationship a habit, preferring to know as little as possible about their sex partners.

And some people waited until a few days before a wedding before revealing how shallow and faithless they truly were, he thought dourly.

Oriel was offering refreshing honesty, a night without the false promises that kept a person dangling on a string. If they were both law-abiding, consenting adults, did it matter why he'd knocked on her door in the first place?

Vijay collected the box of condoms from his luggage and, moments later, knocked on her door again.

"Your concierge request," he said dryly when she let him in.

She blushed, chuckling as she took it, and set it aside. She sobered as she noted he wasn't laughing. "Am I being too presumptuous?"

"Not at all. I want to use one. More than one, if we are so blessed."

That made her laugh throatily, and somehow they were close enough that he snagged his arm around her without thinking. She pressed into him.

He was lost. Any better thoughts went out the covered windows as he folded his arms around her and pressed her curves into his long-term memory. She was all softness and spice, hair spilling around her shoulders as she tipped her head back and showed him the glow of exhilaration in her eyes.

She had taken off her shoes, but was still tall enough that her nose was even with his mouth. Her long, dark throat was more than he could resist. He dipped his head and tasted her skin.

She gasped and shivered, and he automatically closed his arms tighter around her, holding her still for the swirl of his tongue against her skin. How had he thought he could resist her when she responded so immediately? So wantonly. She ran her hands into his hair and arched to rub against the erection straining against his fly.

Slow down, he ordered himself, but they only had tonight, and he wanted every inch of her. She seemed equally urgent, plucking at his shirt until he lifted his mouth and fused his lips to hers.

As they kissed deeply, his pulse throbbed so hard his entire body shook under the reverberations. His hands gathered and roamed over the filmy fabric of her dress, filling his palms with her heat, her lithe waist and her round, firm ass. He had never wanted to rip a woman's clothes off, but the impulse was there tonight. It took everything in him to seek the zipper against the indention of her spine.

"There's a hook," she said as he lowered the tab.

Maybe there was, but he had enough room in the opening to caress the smooth skin above and below the band of her lacy bra.

She flexed and her hand bumped into his, trying to finish opening the dress. She moaned with frustration. "Oh, just break it."

"Thank you," he said fervently, clutching the edge of the zipper and popping the hook. The delicate dress tore in a burst of barbaric satisfaction. He swept the ruined garment forward, peeling it off her front and brushing it down her hips so it landed as a puddle of blue around her feet.

"Mon Dieu," she said on a pang of helpless laughter. "I've never felt like this."

"Me neither." When she began to untuck his shirt, he yanked it open, tearing the cuffs as he roughly pulled it free of his arms, all the while keeping his gaze fixated on the ice-blue lace of her bra and panties.

He may have spent a little too long studying her online photos in skimpy lingerie exactly like that, but reality was even more potent. As he freed his hands from his sleeves, he ran his touch from beneath her arms to her waist and down to her hips before coming back. The soft abrasion of lace against the downy warmth of her skin was a delightful contrast, as was the hint of pink rising beneath her golden skin. He wanted to bite at the dark circles of her areolas, barely visible through the lace in the cups, and *devour* the shadow behind the triangle at the top of her thighs.

"Kiss me." She ran her hands across his bare shoulders and cupped his head, drawing his mouth to hers.

He groaned as he covered her lips and gloried in how her mouth softened in surrender beneath his. He caught her hair and dragged her head back, kissing across her jaw and down to her throat. "I'm going to kiss every part of you," he promised.

Her collarbone, her shoulder where he brushed aside the strap of her bra, the place where her scent gathered between the swells of her breasts.

She opened her bra, and he nearly lost his mind as her breasts spilled into his hands. Her beautiful dark nipples were already pebble-hard as he circled his thumbs across them. He kept swirling his thumb on one while pulling the other deep into his mouth and stabbing at the little bead with his tongue.

A small cry left her, and her hands clutched at him while her weight sagged. His blood throbbed in the tip of his erection, hammering imperatives into his brain.

He ignored his own need and shifted his grip on her, bending her across his arm so he could consume her other nipple. She squirmed, and her helpless pants made him smile with dark satisfaction. When he slid a hand down to silk and discovered it was soaked with her response, he nearly lost it.

"Vijay." Her eyelids were fluttering, and she covered his hand, urging him to press harder.

"Are you going to come?"

"I don't know."

"Let's see, hmm?" He slid a finger under the lace and caressed between her slippery folds, so hot and welcoming. As he dipped his head and found her nipple again, he discovered the hard nub of her clitoris. She stiffened and trembled as he stroked, digging her nails into his scalp. He sucked harder and rolled his touch rhythmically across that little pearl, feeling her quiver and shake.

Her tension gathered until he thought she would break. Suddenly she cried out, shattering so completely, it was like holding a charge of lightning. She electrified him.

Then she went trustingly limp in his embrace, moaning with gratification.

* * *

"That was incredible." Vijay swung her up in the cradle of his arms.

"It was," she murmured, curling a heavy arm around his neck and nuzzling his throat. That orgasm had destroyed her in the most exquisite way. "I can walk," she claimed, even though she wasn't entirely confident in that statement.

"I could carry you to a cave on the top of a mountain right now. Somewhere that no other man will ever find you, so you would be mine forever. All mine. *Only* mine."

She didn't normally find possessiveness sexy, but ooh. She sought his mouth and sucked on his bottom lip. She would be his if he would be hers.

He wouldn't. They only had tonight, she recalled with a catching sensation in her chest.

She might have descended into a fog of despondency then, but he stopped walking to give her a long, luxurious kiss, playing his tongue against hers. When he released her, his dark eyes held a feral glitter.

"Do you mind?"

It took her a moment to realize he wanted her to pick up the box of condoms.

More than one, if we are so blessed.

Oui. Si'l vous plaît. She did, and seconds later, he set her on the bed.

Her gaze snagged on the ceiling fan. She had a brief moment of unease as she recalled they had only met this morning. He had been correct in saying she didn't do one-night stands. Her first sexual experience had been a seduction at the hands of a young man trying to get close to her mother for career reasons. All the rest of her relationships had died of neglect.

Her last attempt at dating had made the complaint, *You're not a virtuoso like your mother. Why does your career mean so much to you?*

In this moment, as Vijay peeled her panties down her thighs as though savoring the opening of a Christmas gift, she realized the reason her career always took precedence was that no man had made her feel like this—cherished and wanted and *necessary*. She was both helpless and powerful, sated yet aroused. Self-conscious, but losing inhibitions by the heartbeat.

"Come here." He dragged her bottom to the edge of the mattress as he lowered to his knees on the floor beside the bed.

"You—I—" She lost her ability to speak as he set her legs on his shoulders and tasted her. No inhibition on his part, either. She groaned in tortured joy as he brought her replete flesh back to searing life.

He drew her to a height of tension, then slowed and soothed, then intensified his ministrations so her need for more became acute again.

"Vijay, please," she begged, and tangled her hands in his hair. "I need you inside me."

"The problem is, my beautiful goddess…" He stood and opened his belt, dropping pants and briefs in one swift skim. "I don't know how long I will last once I'm there."

Oh, he was beautifully made. From the tree of life that decorated his torso to the root of hair that gathered in a nest at the tops of his thighs to the thick spear of flesh dark with arousal. He reached for the condoms, and she watched as he rolled one on and squeezed himself in his fist.

Her body clenched internally with anticipation.

"Yes?" He touched her knee in a request that she open her legs for him.

"Oh, yes." She was dying and scooted herself into the center of the mattress.

He settled over her, bracing on an elbow as he traced the swollen, sheathed head of his penis around her wet entrance.

"Quit teasing." She nipped at his earlobe.

His crown nudged for admittance. He had girth to him. Her body instinctively tensed as his thickness began to invade. She made herself relax, and he pressed into her. All her sensations intensified as he slowly filled her.

"You're so hot," he breathed, backing off slightly before letting his weight settle so he sank to the limits of their flesh.

She had never felt anything like this. Perfectly full. She was so aroused and swollen and sensitized, she could feel his heartbeat in the steeliness lodged within her.

"Your heart is racing," he murmured as he cupped her breast and played with her nipple.

The small caress sent a tight jolt down into the place where they were joined, and she clenched in reaction. Sensations glittered through her, making her catch her breath.

"Like that?" He continued to roll his thumb around her nipple as he kissed her. Long, lazy kisses that drove her mad because her sex was growing wetter and needier, and he used his weight to keep their hips completely still.

She stroked her hands over the curve of his hard buttocks, then twined her legs up around his waist and dug her heels into his hard globes, inviting him to thrust with muted pulses of her hips. She blatantly thrust her tongue into his mouth and arched to encourage him.

He groaned as he rocked back and thrust in, seeming to pull sensations from her like the strings of a harp, then releasing them to send glorious vibrations shivering through her.

She couldn't help the strangled noise that left her. She twisted beneath him, almost overcome by the intensity of the sensations.

"Almost too good to bear, isn't it?" He worked his hand under her tailbone, tilting her hips so he could thrust with more power. As he invaded, he touched places inside her that made her vision go white.

Sharp spears of joy pierced her. It was inescapable, so she embraced it, clinging to him and moving with him, moaning unreservedly. His hand fisted in the sheet beneath her shoulder, and the slap of their hips was a primitive drumbeat beneath the song of their sobs and groans.

Climax licked and teased and tantalized.

"Not yet," he growled. "Wait."

She had never been held like this on the precipice of exaltation. It was exquisite torture. She clutched at him and said filthy things. "Deeper. Harder. Don't stop. I need more."

He kept to that rhythm that was driving her mad, held them in that place of utter abandonment that was too sharp to be withstood, but oh, she wanted to be right here forever.

"Now," he commanded through gritted teeth. *"Come."*

He unleashed himself, pushing her toward the high, wide ledge with unconstrained thrusts. A viscously sweet sensation clenched within her, then released her into the universe, scattering her into pieces.

From a distance, she heard him roar with the force of his own orgasm. He fused his hips to hers and pulsed hotly within her. They stayed locked like that for long, euphoric moments, holding tight to that state of utter perfection before he collapsed upon her, sweaty and heavy and replete.

She sighed, drenched and drugged by a kind of pleasure she had never experienced in her life.

And never would again, she acknowledged with a pang of melancholy.

* * *

"Who was the thief?" the photographer asked as Oriel prepared for her photo shoot the next day.

"What do you mean?" She turned from hanging the robe she'd been wearing over her first bikini.

"The one who left fingerprints on your bottom. We'll have to call the constable to dust them." The photographer winked at his own joke and waved at the makeup artist.

The woman was grinning with amusement as she brought forward a tray of pots in an array of flesh tones from ivory to intense brown and began to mix them like a painter.

Mon Dieu. Oriel wanted to die. The poor woman had already spent an hour trying to disguise the dark circles under her eyes. Now Oriel had to stand here in all her ignominious glory while the sable hairs of a brush tickled the curves of her derriere.

"Don't be embarrassed," the woman said when she rose from her squat and saw Oriel's expression. "Unless he wasn't worth it?"

"Oh, he was," Oriel said ruefully. She had absolutely no regrets. That's what she'd been telling herself as she rose from the bed and had a quick shower a couple of hours ago.

Vijay had been gone when she emerged, but he'd left a note on hotel stationery.

Thank you for an amazing night.

She had his number from the previous note still tucked in a pocket of her bag. She'd been trying to decide if she should text something similar or let last night be a wonderful, stand-alone memory for both of them. Coming on as clingy was the last thing she wanted, but the yearning to keep him in her life was nearly overwhelming. It wasn't that she had felt "complete" with him, but for those hours from dinner through waking beside him, she had stopped feeling so deeply alone.

After several hours of shooting, when she was physically drained and about to change into her own clothes, she took a selfie in the full-length mirror. She was wearing a neon-pink bikini that was almost entirely made of loosely woven strings with a few tiny patches of solid nylon over the important bits.

At the last second, she cut her head out of the photo. Wasn't that the first rule of sexting? Keep it from being too incriminating?

She sent it with a message.

Miss me yet?

Almost immediately, she saw the three dots of a reply.

Niiiice. Who dis?

She texted back.

Not funny.

Then, as it occurred to her that she might have sent it to a wrong number, she asked with growing horror:

Who is this?

Erlich. Send more.

Non, non, non. With a whimper, she turned off her phone, resolving to get a new number the second she arrived back in Paris.

Oriel didn't text him. Which was *fine.* This wasn't his first rodeo, as they said in America. They had agreed their affair would only be the one night, and he'd crossed some ethical boundaries by accepting her invitation.

Vijay had struggled as he lay in her bed listening to the shower come on. He'd considered leaving his card, but decided that slipping away with only a thank-you note had been the most prudent course. If she wanted to reach out to him, she had his number from his earlier note. Leaving it had been a way to explain his stealing her toothbrush and to forestall any awkward involvement of hotel management, but at least she had it.

Three days later, he was still fading into lusty memories of their being all over each other, dozing off their sexual gratification before greedily demanding more. The third time, Oriel had instigated it, reaching for him in the predawn light.

"My alarm will go off soon," she had murmured. "Do you want to…?"

Her caress on the inside of his thigh had been all he needed to recover and harden despite the fact he should have been drained dry. He'd pulled her warm, silky body atop him and filled his hands with her smooth skin while their legs braided together. He'd done his best to memorize her with his touch, letting her set the pace since he imagined she was tender after so much lovemaking.

Her damp mouth and cool hair had drifted a tickling sweep across his chest all the way down to his stomach and lower, anointing him in a way that had him forgetting why breathing was a thing anyone bothered to do.

When she had risen to straddle him and guided herself onto his hardness, he hadn't had a condom on yet, but after that much lovemaking, he had known he wouldn't come right away. He had let her lazily ride him and enjoyed the way she crested with a broken gasp and shivers of ecstasy. Her rippling pleasure on his supremely aroused, sensitized flesh had nearly taken him over the edge, but he'd managed to hold back.

After she calmed, he had slipped out of her, put on a condom and taken control. He'd aroused her with his mouth, making her squirm and writhe. He'd tried to be gentle because they'd been at it for hours, but by the time he was moving inside her, the beast had been gripping him with insatiable talons.

He had known it would be their last time. Each

stroke had been bittersweet. Powerful. They had completely abandoned propriety, both moaning and encouraging the other until the people in the next room had banged on the wall and yelled, "Give it a rest!"

He couldn't. He had wanted to meld them into one being for all time. Parting from her was going to leave a piece of himself behind. When the culmination arrived, he'd nearly blacked out from the force—

"Vijay!"

His sister's voice snapped him back to his office. He shifted in his chair, arousal dying a quick death as he leaned to see her across the small courtyard they shared. They left their doors open for exactly this, so they could call across whenever they had a question.

Kiran was glaring at him.

"Are you worried about the language around the patent? Me too." They'd both been studying the offer from TecSec. At least, that's what he was supposed to be doing.

"Why is Jalil texting from the coffee shop, asking me if I want a chai latte and whether I'll be sitting in on his meeting with *you*?" Kiran demanded.

"Is he here? We can do it in your office if you like."

He rose and walked through the courtyard. It was really just a short hallway with a skylight and a water feature against the back wall to provide some cooling and atmospheric noise.

The rest of their company offices were on this

same ground floor of a four-story, glass-fronted commercial building. It looked onto an abstract sculpture and a collection of taller buildings. At the far end was the café where Jalil bought Kiran coffee. Above them was an architecture firm, a publishing agency, and a call center for a company in America.

They hoped to take over all of that once the acquisition went through because this was such a good space for Kiran's wheelchair, but they would also open a center in Delhi before looking to Singapore, Hong Kong and Shanghai over the next few years.

"What is this about?" She watched him close the courtyard doors with a glower of suspicion.

"Just a quick hand of poker."

"Is this why you disappeared for a few days on your way home from Europe?" She narrowed her eyes. "Look, just because I haven't found proof that Lakshmi visited a clinic while she was away, doesn't mean anything. A clinic like that would be very discrete about how they handled their records. Twenty-five years ago, they might have still been using paper."

Vijay didn't have to respond. There was a knock, and Jalil was shown in. He was a healthy widower of fiftysomething with strands of silver in his otherwise thick black hair. He held a cardboard tray of three disposable cups.

As he and Kiran saw one another, the pair lit up and smiled and shared a look of tangled emotions that was so intimate, Vijay had to look away.

He had thought he had that once, the feeling of

someone else's emotions being his own. It had been a lie, and he was not looking forward to picking up the pieces when Kiran realized Jalil was toying with her.

Actually, he had thought he might have something like it with Oriel, too, but her silence spoke volumes. Sexual connection was simply that, a trick of biology, and he wouldn't allow Jalil to use it on his sister.

He couldn't wait to expose the man and kick him out of their lives once and for all.

"Vijay, Kiran said you like black coffee." Jalil's warm smile turned stiff. He set the tray on the corner of her desk and pulled out each cup.

Kiran and Vijay provided a well-stocked break room full of coffee, tea and soft drinks for their staff, but Jalil liked to impress Kiran by overpaying for takeaway.

This was what annoyed Vijay about the man. He could have kept his pursuit of his "niece" entirely professional, but he hadn't.

Did you?

Oh, shut up, Vijay told the irritating voice in his head.

"It was kind of you to think of me," Vijay said as politely as he could. "And thank you for coming in." He waved at a chair in invitation, waiting until Jalil had seated himself before saying, "I have good news." Jalil wouldn't see it that way, but Vijay certainly did. "While I was in Europe, I was able to intercept Oriel Cuvier and get a DNA sample—"

"You *told* her?" Kiran cried.

"No. I stole her toothbrush and sent it to the lab we use. I didn't put her name on the paperwork. It's Sample X, but Jalil can offer his own sample, and we can put an end to speculation." Vijay leaned on Kiran's desk, facing Jalil. He crossed his arms and ankles and conveyed a silent and ruthless *checkmate*.

"I can't believe you would jeopardize Jalil's confidentiality." Kiran rolled out from behind the desk to move next to Jalil. "I am *so* sorry I told him what you had asked me to do."

"Don't be," Jalil said, patting Kiran's arm in a placating way. "Your brother has gone to a lot of trouble on my behalf."

Vijay had absolutely not done it for Jalil's benefit, and they all knew it. He was trying to get rid of a man who was playing his sister.

"I know it must seem as though I'm grasping at straws," he said to Vijay. "You have every right to be skeptical of my motives, but this is something I've wondered every day since Lakshmi returned from Europe. When I saw those photos of Ms. Cuvier and read up on her details, I couldn't stop thinking about this possibility, but I didn't know how to ask her without tipping my hand. I would be devastated if Lakshmi's reputation was tarnished by false rumors. This is perfect. Thank you. How do I proceed?"

"You want to give a sample?" Vijay tried not to let his jaw hit the floor.

"Of course."

Vijay had just had his own bluff called.

CHAPTER FOUR

WORST. IDEA. EVER.

Duke Rhodes hadn't booked her into a hotel. He'd added Oriel to the roster of guests on a yacht. Granted, it was a billionaire's superyacht and was full to the gunwales with entertainment industry movers and shakers as well as artists and designers. Oriel even knew a handful of them *and* she'd been given her own stateroom—not that she was in it.

Payton had instructed her to use this to her advantage. *See and be seen.* Easier said than done when Duke wanted her by his side like a security blanket.

At least he wasn't being a creep about it. He had looped his arm around her as they walked the red carpet, keeping it colleague-friendly, not pervy, but she had still hated it.

She was so burnt out, she felt like charred bacon. She had been working nonstop for weeks, putting in long days and getting most of her sleep on airplanes crisscrossing the Atlantic. She was beyond ready for vacation, but she had to paste a smile on her face and pretend to be thrilled with Duke's latest film—which struck her as a paint-by-numbers rehash of every action flick ever made. The audience's tepid response seemed to agree.

By the time they arrived back on the yacht, the after-party was in full swing.

Oriel wished she had confessed to the headache that was intensifying behind her brow. It was growing bad enough to make her nauseous.

Duke was holding court, though, drinking and smoking and making off-color jokes. He wasn't a terrible person so much as a man in denial of his age. He wanted to be twenty, so that's how he was acting. He loved his cigarettes, which he lit with a shaking hand, making her suspect he had social anxiety, but the smell was turning her stomach.

Either way, all her years of practicing aloof, unbothered looks were being severely tested as Duke blathered on about his glory days.

"I need the powder room," she murmured and excused herself.

She needed to find a tender to run her to shore. She was flying home to her parents' in the morning and had overheard someone say the yacht was hauling anchor at first light. Why had she agreed to this wretched stunt?

She texted Payton as she moved into the crush of the saloon, telling him she was done with this pageantry, and asked if he knew of any rooms she could book at this late hour.

What happened? I told his people this was only for publicity. If he's crossed a line, tell me. I don't put my clients in harm's way.

Oriel didn't feel like explaining that pretending to be with Duke made her feel cheap. It made her think about everything he wasn't. About *who* he wasn't and who she really wanted to spend her time with.

Not that the man she *did* want had reached out in the nearly two months since they'd spent their rapturous night in Milan. Granted, she'd been on the move, but she wasn't hard to reach. She could be contacted online fairly easily.

Maybe he'd given her the wrong number on purpose. That's what she kept thinking. He could have given her his number again with that second note, but he hadn't. She was the ultimate feminine stooge who had fallen for a player's game, and it made her feel like an absolute neophyte.

She caught up to a steward, who told her she only needed to go down to the lower deck in the stern where she had come aboard. A tender was making regular trips to shore all night.

She moved down a staircase to the passageway that led to her room and halted. A man in a dark suit stood outside the door to her room.

Mon Dieu, he looked just like Vijay.

Her heart screeched to a stop in her chest while such a rush of joy exploded in her, she had to reach back and grasp the rail to stay upright. At the same time, her mind blared an alarm at how *not normal* it was that he would be here.

It had been nearly two months to the day since she'd met him. Slept with him. He'd been on her mind every day, but when the number he'd given her turned out to be wrong, she'd decided they weren't meant to be.

Or that he had never really wanted them to be. How had he known where to find her? Bumping into him in a restaurant a few blocks from her hotel had been unexpected, but a reasonable happenstance. Of all the yachts in the south of France right now, however, he was on this one? Standing outside her door?

No, he must have come to find her, but how had he gotten on board? Given all the celebrities in attendance, security was very tight. He had some sort of security company, she recalled vaguely, but it still seemed very odd.

As she stood there trying to assimilate his presence, he turned his head.

"Oriel." His voice pierced as sharply as his flaring gaze.

His innate energy leaped down the long passageway to catch at her, threatening to overwhelm her the way he had the first time. It was so visceral, it alarmed her. She hadn't properly gotten over him, and here he was about to make it worse.

Acting purely on instinct, she whirled around and fled up the stairs like Cinderella from the ball. She didn't know why she needed to get away. She just did.

She tried to, anyway.

"Sweetheart. Where you going?" Duke lurched in front of her, swaying, eyes barely open.

Oriel tugged Duke out a door so they stood at the rail and dredged up a lame smile.

"This has been so much fun." *Lie*. "But I have an early flight tomorrow. I'm going to get a room on shore."

"What's the problem, sugar? Feeling neglected?" Duke splayed a hand on her waist. "I can't help it if I'm popular. C'mon. We'll go to my room."

"What? Ew. *No*." She tried to brush his hand off her, but he caught hers and wouldn't let her shake him off. *"Duke."*

People further along the rail turned their heads.

He crowded into her, cajoling, "Don't make me look bad, sweetheart."

Good heavens, was he begging? What a poor, desperate man.

She looked him straight in the eye and said, "You need rehab. Do you want me to ask my agent to arrange it if yours won't?"

He dismissed that with a tired curse, hissing, "I need good press, darling. Come to my room. Let people think what they think. That's all I want. Swear."

"No." She pressed his chest, but he kept her trapped against the rail. "Seriously, Duke. Back off. Let me go."

"Come *on*. I got you a room so you'd at least *pretend* we're having sex."

"I'll see that you're given a full refund," she muttered and pushed harder. *"Let me go."*

Duke was suddenly yanked back a few steps.

"I will cut you up and throw you to the sharks," Vijay said in the most frightening tone Oriel had ever heard.

"Vijay!" She shot out a protesting hand.

Before she could react further, security guards emerged from the shadows and closed in on all of them. They clapped their hands on Vijay, forcing him to release Duke.

"I know him," she blurted, still holding up her hand as if she had some kind of magical powers to stop men from acting like barbarians. *"Tout va bien."* Was it fine? Maybe Vijay was some sort of stalker who had followed her here. She didn't know.

"I'm Vijay Sahir. I work for TecSec. Let me go." Vijay tried to shrug off the men holding him. "I'll show you my card. You can call in for my credentials."

Confusion ensued. Duke spat venom in her direction about bitches being crazy, and staggered off. Oriel and Vijay were invited to quit ruining the party and wait in her stateroom until Vijay's identity was confirmed.

Oriel could have balked at being left alone with him. His presence here was growing more bizarre by the second. Her parents used TecSec. Were they okay?

He was the only one with answers, so she led him into her stateroom. It was a midrange one with built-in shelves, recessed lighting, and a double bed. The shades were pulled over the windows, and she hadn't bothered to unpack, so her suitcase was open on the rack.

Somehow, she had wound up with one of Vijay's cards in her hand.

"This says Vice President of TecSec Asia Division." At least one mystery was explained. She had mistaken a five for an eight when she had texted him her bikini photo. "You made it sound as though you were barely scraping by." Why else would he have been working in maintenance at the hotel?

"I told you we had a deal in the works that I couldn't talk about. Are you all right? Did he hurt you?" He noted she was massaging her wrist and carefully took her forearm in his two hands.

His touch. It was as beguiling as ever, sending little tingles of awareness all through her.

She made herself pull away and step back. It took everything in her not to let him see how thrown she was by his turning up this way. How defenseless he made her feel. Her whole body felt electrified. *Awake.* Which undermined her confidence, because she didn't want to be this sensitive and reliant on anyone, least of all a man who had stripped her down to her most elemental self and seemed like he could effortlessly do it again.

"I'm fine." She might bruise later, but only because when Duke had released her, she had snapped her hand back so hard she'd bumped her wrist on the rail. "Why are you here?"

"They wouldn't let me near you at the premiere, but fans of Rhodes tipped me off to the fact you were staying on board with him here. I swear, the best security system in the world is no match for autograph seekers," he said ironically. "This yacht is leaving for Italy in the morning, though. I didn't want to miss you."

He was different than she recollected. His hair was a little shorter, his tailored suit on par with those of the movie stars and producers continuing their gaiety beyond these walls. His expression was forbidding, though. Nothing like the easygoing man she'd taken him for.

Or the humble maintenance man he had pretended to be.

"How did you know I was in Cannes? Are *you* some kind of super fan?" Worse? "Have you been spying on me? Tracking my phone?" She glanced around for it as if it would be glowing with a beacon.

"Nothing that high-tech." He was still using that dry tone. "I overheard your conversation in Milan. You said this trip would cut into your vacation. I thought it would be a good idea for you to have personal time after we talk."

"That's very arrogant."

"Which part? Assuming how you'll react to what I have to say?" His voice hardened. "Or that you would speak to me at all?"

That took her aback until she recalled that she had run the minute she'd seen him.

All this time, she had been telling herself she was

fine with not hearing from him. It was what they had agreed on, but deep down, she'd taken it as a rejection, one that stuck like a thorn in her heart.

As sophisticated as she'd tried to be about their night together, she'd also been more uninhibited with him than she'd ever been in her life. That knowledge kept hitting her in ever stronger waves as she remained in his presence, like a tide coming in. Her self-consciousness was deepening by the minute, and her feet were stuck in the sand. She wanted to get away, but couldn't.

Meanwhile, he stood there with his Just The Facts Ma'am attitude, suggesting he barely remembered they'd clung to each other while moaning with abject passion.

"I was surprised to see you," she said with as much dignity as she could scrape together. "Why didn't you reach out through my website or my social profiles?"

"You had my number but didn't reach out," he said with a negligent shrug. "I wasn't sure you would take my call, and this is important."

She wanted to say, *You gave me the wrong number*, but if this card was anything to go by, he'd given her the wrong everything.

"Why were you working for that hotel in Milan? Were you actually in their security department?"

He licked his lips, the first sign of him not feeling completely in control of this moment. "We hope that hotel will join our roster of clients. I presented to them while I was there, but no. I was not working for them in any capacity when I met you."

"Then why…?" She was growing deeply uneasy, pinching his card so hard her thumbnail went white.

"I told you the truth when I said I was trying to prove something to my sister." His detached air cracked enough that his cheek ticked. "As it turns out, she was right and I was wrong."

How much did it cost him to admit that? she wondered with a twinge of grim amusement.

"What is that supposed to mean? What are you doing here? What were you doing there?" She could feel hysteria edging into her psyche. It made her sick that he'd had some sort of ulterior motive when they'd made love. It sullied her memory of a night that was otherwise pure and wonderful. It made her feel used. Not desired for herself.

Unwanted.

He flicked open his jacket as if he was overheating.

Despite how fractious this moment was, she became acutely aware of his flat stomach and had a flashing vision of kissing across his muscled abdomen while her breasts nestled his erection. He'd tangled his hands in her hair and groaned as if she was torturing him in the most exquisite way possible.

A searing mix of arousal and embarrassment poured through her. She had been utterly shameless with him. It had felt right at the time, as if they were both revealing something no one else had ever reached, but now her gaze pinned itself to the floor, mortified.

A sudden knock rapped before the door swung open, making her gaze fly up in a panicked *What now?* One of the ship's security guards strode in and handed Vijay the passport he'd taken from him a few minutes ago.

"Thank you for your patience, sir. You're free to go anytime. Please let me know if I can assist in any way."

"Thank you." Vijay pocketed his passport and nodded at the door in arrogant dismissal. The man left, closing the door behind him.

Oriel stared at the closed door, wondering if she should be reassured by the deference that man had shown or intimidated. She clung to her elbows.

"Are my parents okay? Does this have something to do with them?"

"Not in the way you think. To the best of my knowledge, your mother and father are completely fine. But you should sit down." Vijay pulled out the chair tucked beneath the built-in desk. "What I'm going to tell you will shock you. It's about your birth family."

Oriel instinctively backed away. She was already against a wall, though. Some kind of knob was trying to puncture her kidney. She barely felt it. Her hair scraped against the wood as she shook her head.

"I know all I need to about them."

His face blanked with shock. "You do?"

"Yes." Oriel repeated what she had always known.

"They were a mixed race couple, and that was a problem for my birth mother's family, so she gave me up." Which cut Oriel to the bone, obviously, but not everyone enjoyed the advantages she and her parents had. She tried not to judge her biological mother too harshly, not when she didn't have all the facts. "I've never wanted to cause problems to resurface for them, so I've never tried to find them. Plus, it would hurt my parents if they thought I was looking for my birth family. So, no thank you. Keep whatever you know to yourself."

Despite her dignified refusal, her heart pounded so hard she thought her ribs would crack. Her stomach was seriously trying to turn itself inside out.

Vijay set his hands on his hips. He started to speak a few times before finally saying, "I've been thinking about this from every angle, trying to work out how to phrase things. It never once occurred to me you wouldn't want to hear it. But okay." He nodded with bewilderment. "That's your choice." He rubbed his jaw, casting about the room as though completely at sea. "You have my card if you change your mind."

He looked at the card she held. In her agitation, she had twisted it beyond recognition. He removed a fresh one from his pocket and set it on the folded clothes inside her suitcase.

He stood there a long moment, staring at her.

A million images flashed into her mind, from his first sexy side-eye when he had entered her suite to his quick smile at the bar. The way the touch of his leg against her own had filled her with melting heat, and with a cocky brow, he declared they were on a date. His kisses and caresses and deeply generous lovemaking and his note that had claimed it had been an amazing night.

She waited for him to acknowledge any of that, but he only nodded once and said, "Good night." He started for the door.

"That's it?" she cried, panic-stricken that he would walk away so easily. *Again.* "You can't just stroll back into my life with a baited hook and dangle it like that! What were you trying to prove?"

"To my sister? You just said you don't want to know."

She pressed back into the wall again. "If you tell me you and I are related…"

"No," he choked out. His mouth twitched, but he added firmly, "Absolutely not."

She hugged herself, searching his eyes for clues. Until this moment, she would have sworn that she had no interest in learning about her birth parents. She had long ago made peace with the fact she would never know more about where she came from than she'd always known.

She suddenly discovered she did have questions, though. Thousands of them, each one making her burn with curiosity. There was a scorch of guilt that came with it. This desire to hear more felt disloyal to the people who had always treated her as though they'd made her themselves.

"I love my parents," she blurted.

"I'm sure you do." His voice gentled. "This is my mistake, Oriel. It's been a busy few weeks for my company. I got it into my head that I had to have all of that wrapped up so I could catch you here in Cannes before you went on vacation, but you're right. This is something you should learn in your own way on your own timeline. It's just…" His gaze flickered down her silver gown, which was covered in sequins that caught the light. "Well, it was good to see you again. Call if you want to talk to me."

"Why didn't they just write to me? What about an email?" She threw up a flailing arm. "Have they *always* known where I was?" The thought of that nearly broke her into pieces. Who kept something like that from someone? "Why didn't you warn me that you were planning to come back into my life with news like this? Why are *you* the one delivering this news? *Mon Dieu*, is that why you sought me out in Milan?"

It was. She knew it as she said it. Her heart hardened into a stony lump in her chest. She had thought she was special, that they had shared something extraordinary. But she had never been special. Not special enough. Not good enough to keep.

"The situation is delicate." His cheeks hollowed. "Best handled personally so things can be managed on both ends. I don't want to say more than that because you've just said you don't want to know."

"Who do you think you are?" she cried, charging forward a few steps. "You've come all this way. I'm not going to let you torture me with it. *Tell me.*"

He stiffened as though bracing for a physical attack. His head went back and he looked down his nose, but otherwise he was very still.

"Are you sure, Oriel? There's no going back—"

"Vijay." A pulsing charge was running through her, burning painfully in her arteries, throbbing and stinging and making her stomach swish around and around. She thought she might throw up, but fought it back, glaring at him. Daring him to speak or walk out. She didn't even know what was worse right now, looking into his eyes knowing he didn't care about her, or letting him walk away with her deepest secrets still unlocked.

He seemed to hold every part of her in his wide hand. Did he realize that?

After an interminable silence, he nodded at the chair. "You look like you're going to snap in half."

Sitting down felt like lowering herself onto a bed of nails. Her whole body was prickling with confusion, wanting to react to something big without knowing what it was. She clutched her hands together and pressed them to her trembling lips, probably most infuriated by the fact he was witnessing her react this nakedly.

"My adoption is supposed to be *my* information," she told him resentfully. "*I* should decide who I share it with and how much is known. You're not supposed to come here and tell me things I don't know about myself. Not things that are so…" the word *intimate* wasn't strong enough "…*integral* to who I am."

"You're right."

She instantly hated him for that ultra-reasonable tone. It told her how badly she was betraying herself if he thought she was in danger of a breakdown and had to neutralize her emotions by sounding all calm and agreeable.

Bitter tears stood in her eyes as she watched him lower to the corner of the bed. He set his elbows on his knees and linked his hands loosely. His expression was very grave.

"It's not much of a defense, but I didn't believe this theory would prove true. It seemed too outrageous. I went to Milan thinking I would prove to my sister she was being fed a fabrication."

"Kiran," she recollected. "You thought someone was trying to take advantage of her."

"Yes. Because reuniting lost families isn't something we even do, but this man had seen your photo and thought you looked like his sister. The timing of your birth matched a trip she'd taken to Europe a few years before she passed away."

"She's dead." A cold wind buffeted her, pushing her back into her chair. She had to take a measured breath to absorb what a blow that news was. She really had been carrying a lot of unacknowledged maybes and somedays. Tears of grief and loss gathered in her throat.

Vijay waited until she lifted her gaze.

"I'm sorry." He offered his hand. "Do you want me to give you a few minutes?"

"No," she choked and tucked her cold, bloodless hands between her knees.

"I'll tell you up front that I have no idea who your birth father is. He remains a mystery, but our client saw your photos and recalled some remarks his sister had made. He became convinced you were his biological niece. I thought he was using the mystery to spend time with Kiran, and the sooner I proved him wrong, the sooner he would leave her alone." He paused as though giving her a chance to brace herself. "I went to your room in Milan so I could steal your toothbrush. I sent it to a DNA lab."

"You're not allowed to do that," she hissed, sitting up straighter. "You're supposed to get a person's consent."

"It was expensive," he allowed with a tilt of his head. "I didn't attach your name to it. I thought the man was a fraud, Oriel. I thought I would force him to admit he was blowing smoke and make him disappear. Or he'd go through with the test, it wouldn't match, and I could tell him to go to hell for sending us on a wild goose chase. I didn't expect it would lead back to you. And I never once took for granted what I was doing was crossing a line. I am sorry."

"It matches?" Of course it did, or he wouldn't be here.

Her stomach tightened, and she pushed herself deeper into the chair. On some higher plane she was appalled that Vijay had gone behind her back. She would never forgive him for interfering in her life in such an underhanded way, but her eyes were fixated on his mouth, her ears straining for every word.

"He's...my uncle?"

"It came back with a high statistical likelihood that you're related, yes. You look a *lot* like his sister, Lakshmi Dalal. She was a very famous Bollywood star around the time you were born."

"No." Oriel dismissed it on reflex. "My birth parents were from Romania and Turkey. I was born at a private clinic in Luxembourg."

"Lakshmi went to Europe with her manager about four months before you were born, supposedly to record some songs at a private studio. When she came back, she was different. Her brother could tell she was grieving. He believes her manager pressured her to give up her baby for the sake of her career."

"Is he still alive? The manager? Has anyone *asked* him?"

"Jalil is being very careful. He's afraid the manager, Gouresh Bakshi, will attack you and smear Lakshmi's memory. Or he'll lie or line his own pockets by selling some version of the story. Jalil would love more answers, but he doesn't believe he would get the truth from that man. He hoped you or your parents might have some piece of the story. Would you be willing to speak to him?"

"Go to India?"

"Or video chat. Take as much time as you need to think about that."

"I don't need to think." She shook her head and rose. Adrenaline was pouring into her system, and her mind fixated on one thing. "I need to go home. I need to see my parents."

She needed to go to ground like a wounded animal. Her mind was too shocked to form any other thought. She began to gather her few items scattered around the room as though she could outrun the crazed hurt and anguish breathing on her neck and sending trickles of apprehension down her spine.

She couldn't make sense of what this might mean and wouldn't even try. Better to carry on with her original plan.

"Oriel." Vijay tried to catch her by the hands. "You're in shock."

"Oh, don't pretend you care!" She shook him off. "Really, Vijay? Really? This is the reason you slept with me? To steal a toothbrush and ruin my life? Go to hell!"

CHAPTER FIVE

SHE SWEPT AROUND him with a rustle of her sparkling gown. The graze of her sequined skirt against his leg was an absent caress that wafted a tortuous sensuality through him.

How had he forgotten how truly beautiful she was? He'd let his memory of her harden and dull, telling himself he was better off because she hadn't tried to stay in contact. They were too far apart in more ways than geography. If she was the kind who resorted to publicity stunts to advance her career, she wasn't that different from Wisa. He definitely didn't need anyone like that in his life again.

Despite that very sensible conclusion, from the second he had confirmed Jalil was her blood uncle, Vijay had been anticipating seeing Oriel again. Jalil had still been speechless and pale when Vijay had urged him not to make any moves without discussing it with him. He'd confessed to having dinner with Oriel, not the rest, but insisted on being the one to inform her.

He had told himself he simply wanted to come

clean about his part in this discovery, that it was the decent thing to do, but he'd been impatient to see her again. His heart had leaped into his throat when he'd seen her at the end of the passageway. The animal within him had finally scented his mate.

He didn't know what he had expected, but not that she would turn and *run*.

His gut tightened at that memory of her dress swirling and disappearing up the stairs. It had stung, damn it. But had he really thought she would be happy to see him? She was probably mortified she had slept with a commoner.

Moments later, when he'd found Duke cornering her, he'd been overcome with rage. The actor was lucky he hadn't been thrown into the sea.

That sharp swing of emotions had been so unsettling, he had steeled himself to stick to the facts once they were alone.

Then she had astonished him by refusing to hear him out. It hadn't computed when he'd spent weeks thinking, *I have to get to her. I have to explain.*

He had expected her to be shocked. Anyone would be, but as someone whose beliefs about his own parents had been shattered when he had least expected it, he should have realized she would be shaken to her core.

The way she was trembling and seemed greenish-gray beneath her natural tan alarmed him.

"Will you sit down and give yourself a minute?"

"No." She clapped her case closed and thumped it onto the floor, then yanked up the retractable handle with a snap. She scooped up her shoulder bag, checked its contents, then slung it across her body before snagging her case and starting through the door.

Vijay caught the door and followed her through it.

"You're really leaving?" He set his hand on the handle of her suitcase.

She held on and crashed her furious gaze into his.

As their knuckles sat against one another's, a deeply vulnerable glint edged into her eyes. It slid like a knife between his ribs, parting his lips on a sharp inhale. He had made a grave error. She was more than shaken. She was devastated.

"Oriel." He didn't know what else to say.

Her brow flinched, and she snatched her hand away, saying caustically, "Fine. Be my valet. Saves me the trouble of carrying it." She swished ahead of him. "But then you can go to hell."

"So you already suggested."

The throng of party guests in a small bar turned their heads as he and Oriel strode through, trading barbs. Vijay paused to get his bearings, then redirected her down some steps to water level.

"Transport to shore, please," Oriel said to the deckhand when they arrived.

"The tender just left." The young man nodded at the running lights disappearing toward the glow of the city. "It will be back in thirty or forty minutes."

"My boat is right here." Vijay moved to where his rented speedboat was tied and set her suitcase inside it.

Oriel was a Victorian queen in that stunning dress with her hair teased up in loops. Earrings like chandeliers dangled, while she was nude from her chin down her long neck to that plunging point between her breasts. She stood with her arms straight at her sides, likely hiding clenched fists in the folds of her skirt while she glared at him in a way that declared, *Off with his head.*

Waves were hitting the yacht from all sides, causing sucking and slurping noises. The deck lifted and fell. He saw her swallow uncertainly.

"Wait for the tender if you want. I'll wait with you." It wasn't a warning, more of a promise.

"Oh—" She strung together some very un-regal words and gathered her skirts. "I'm only going with you because it's the quickest way to get to shore and away from you."

He helped her into his tender and handed her a PFD.

"You can't get me to dry land without drowning me along the way?"

"You're wearing chain mail. If you fall overboard, you're sinking straight to the bottom. It's dark out." He didn't even want to contemplate trying to make such a rescue. "Is the gown rented?" He would have to make arrangements to return it.

"It was a gift."

"From Duke?"

She shoved her arms into the vest and closed the tabs, then lowered herself onto the seat nearest her suitcase, chin high, nose turned to the water.

Very well, then. Vijay shrugged into his own vest and started the engine, nodding at the deckhand to cast him off while he sent a quick text to ensure his car would be waiting.

Was he jealous of her wearing something another man had given her? He was so green he was septic with it. He had been from the moment he had learned she wasn't staying in a hotel but was on this yacht with the dissolute actor. At least there'd been no evidence of Duke sharing that stateroom with her, but what did he know?

What right did he have to care? None. Oriel had made clear she had no further interest in him when she hadn't reached out to him after their night. *Which was fine.* They had agreed it was a one-time thing. She didn't belong to him.

Oriel made a noise behind him, and he glanced back to see her grasp at the side of the boat as they hit a patch of wash that made for a bumpy ride. He eased off the throttle.

A metaphor for how he ought to handle her?

What was left to handle? He'd gone behind her back, and she was furious with him. The fact that he was still sexually enthralled by her meant nothing.

They arrived at the marina, and he helped her onto the dock once the boat was secured. He could feel how her hand was shaking. Her expression looked anguished.

"Are you all right?"

"Fine." She spat the word like it was poison.

He returned the keys for the boat, and she paused next to him to ask the man in the rental shack if there was a shuttle service to a hotel.

"I have a car waiting," Vijay told her.

"Good for you. I'll make my own way." She wrested the handle of her suitcase from him and rolled it toward the bottom of the ramp that led up to the parking lot.

"Do you have a room booked? Because the entire world has checked into the city for the film festival." He was staying in a middling three-star place well back from the bay where the only window looked onto the pool.

"Do you know what's funny?" She whirled to face him. "The day we met, when I let you into my room, my agent said that was how lives were ruined. I should have listened to him."

She spun away and started up the ramp. Her suitcase caught on the lip. She turned and roughly gave it a yank, trying to make it come with her, but it was well hooked. She released a noise of helpless fury and shook it harder.

Vijay moved to help, but she released it so abruptly, it tumbled back onto his legs. He barely managed to keep from losing his footing and falling into the water.

"Look," he said shortly. "We need a reset before one of us—"

Oriel grasped the rail on the ramp and leaned over it, moaning with pain.

"Oriel!" He left the suitcase on the dock and hurried up the ramp to set his arms on either side of her. "Are you going to faint? What's wrong?"

She lost her stomach over the rail into the shallow water below.

Ah, hell. He smoothed a few tendrils of her hair away from her face and neck and rubbed her back until she finished retching.

"Mon Dieu," she moaned, sagging against the rail. "How is this night getting worse?"

He offered the black silk of his pocket square. "You get seasick." Or was this a visceral reaction to him and his news?

Vijay had a pigheaded view that ignorance was not bliss. Once he'd learned about his father's crimes, he'd been eaten up by guilt that he hadn't at least made enquiries sooner.

He had twisted his contempt for himself and his own willful blindness into thinking Oriel not only had a right to know about Lakshmi, but that she *needed* to know. If Lakshmi's manager forced Oriel's adoption, he couldn't be allowed to get away with it!

He was conveniently forgetting the hours of ruminating and soul-searching he'd done getting to the decisions he'd made and the actions he'd taken.

Oriel wiped her mouth and straightened, still trembling.

"Let me take you to my hotel," he said gently. "If they don't have a room, we'll ask them to phone around. Either way, you'll be comfortable while we sort things out." He went back for her case, then set his arm around her to guide her up the ramp. "I didn't mean to cause you this much distress."

"What did you think would happen?" she asked with disbelief.

"That it would go slightly less poorly than this."

"You lied to get me into bed."

"No—" As they arrived in the parking lot, his car slid to a stop at the curb. He opened the door. She sank into the back seat, still pale and subdued.

He closed the privacy screen as the limo worked its way into the knot of bumper-to-bumper traffic.

"Oriel." He squeezed his thighs so he wouldn't reach for her. "I honestly thought it wouldn't be true. Everything we said about not having another opportunity to be together was real. I never expected to see you again."

"So you took advantage of the one chance you had to nail me? That makes it all better, then." She helped herself to a miniature bottle of water.

"I didn't seduce you."

"You *lied*."

"I kept one detail from you because I wasn't at liberty to reveal it." He held up a finger, aware this angry defensiveness was the diametric opposite from the way he'd planned to handle this. He was supposed to be giving her the sincere apology she rightfully deserved, but clipped excuses were spewing out of him instead. "If you hadn't been Lakshmi's daughter, I couldn't risk starting rumors that she potentially had one. I didn't know you would come to that restaurant. You invited me to eat with you. You invited me to your room after. Remember? *Bring condoms*, you said."

"Well, I regret that now, don't I?"

"Only now?" he asked with more bitterness than he meant to reveal.

She snapped her head around. "What is that supposed to mean?"

"The second you saw me tonight, you turned and ran."

"Because I was *embarrassed*. You ghosted me."

"No, I didn't." He frowned. "You had my number."

"You have terrible handwriting," she spat, then looked toward the window. "I sent a bikini pic to a stranger because of you, thanks very much. I had to change my number."

She was speaking contemptuously, blaming him, but he was grimly thrilled to hear she had made an effort to reach out.

"I was completely sincere with my second note." He spoke more calmly. "The attraction I felt was real. I enjoyed being with you that night."

"I hate to break it to you, Vijay, but a lot of men are attracted to me. That doesn't mean they get to sleep with me under false pretenses."

His temperature skyrocketed, but he bit his tongue because the car was arriving at his hotel. There was no doorman, so the chauffeur slipped around to open her door while Vijay climbed out his own. As he came around to her side, he saw Oriel grasp at the edge of the door. She had gone white and looked like she was going to throw up again.

He hurried to get his arm around her.

She pressed a weak hand against his chest, obviously resenting that she had to lean on him, but she needed his support.

He managed to tip the driver and take charge of her case, but as the car drove away, he kept her in the fresh night air.

"Is this something more serious? Bad shellfish? A bug?"

"I don't know," she said plaintively. "I thought it was Duke's cigarette smoke and being on the boat that was making me feel so awful. I haven't eaten much today."

"I'll order room service." He guided her into one of the pockets of the revolving door, saying facetiously, "You're not pregnant, are you?"

They both halted.

The door bumped them from behind, nudging them into the bustling noise of the lobby.

He looked down at her sallow face. Her eyes were swallowing up her features.

A dry lump formed in his throat. A nest of cobras arrived in his stomach.

"Are you?" His lips felt numb. A vivid memory came to him of the exquisite sensation when she'd been riding his naked flesh. He hadn't come, though. Even if he had, surely he'd have been shooting blanks by then!

"No. That's—no, of course not." She didn't sound

sure. She looked aghast, but who wouldn't after the last few hours? "No. That would be ridiculous."

I hate to break it to you, Oriel, but "ridiculous" was left behind long ago.

He didn't say it. He led her to the elevator and walked her to his room, experiencing a twinge of embarrassment when he let her in. The room was clean and secure, but it was no superyacht or even the classy place they'd stayed at in Milan.

"It's all I could get at the last minute." And he'd thought it would be only him.

"It's fine." She dropped her shoulder bag on the bed and moved to the window, where she hugged herself while staring down at the guests partying alongside the pool.

"Do you..." He pushed his hands into his pockets. "Do you want me to go to a pharmacy?"

"No." Her fingernails were digging into her upper arm. "But I think you should." Her gaze flashed over to his, swiping through him like a blade when he saw the deeply apprehensive shadows lurking there. "Just to be sure."

He tried again to swallow the lump in his throat. His lungs felt tight. He nodded, glad to have an excuse to catch a breath of air and organize his thoughts.

"Order something," he said, nodding at the card on the nightstand. "Maybe you just need to settle your stomach."

Her eyes widened with persecution, as if food was one decision too many.

"I'll ask downstairs, have something sent up," he offered.

"Thank you." She was staring at the pool again.

The fact she was not throwing sarcasm and defiant looks at him said a lot. She was worried. Which worried him.

Did it? He didn't know what to think or feel.

He moved like a robot, asked for directions at the registration desk, and almost forgot to request two bowls of soup be sent to his room.

What if Oriel was pregnant? Was it even his? If it was, what would he do?

At one time he had assumed without question that he would eventually marry and become a father. His parents had been indulgent, his broader family of aunts, uncles and cousins a warm network of affection, endless food and constant laughter. The expectation of a similar life had been very natural—if intimidating when his grandmother had dubbed him "man of the house" after his parents' death. Vijay had had her and Kiran to look after, though, and his father's business to take over. He had focused on growing into the role and had been determined to do it well.

When the foundations of the business proved to be rotten and his fiancée's fidelity was revealed to be equally compromised, Vijay had put aside aspirations of marriage and parenting. Staying clothed and fed had become his priority.

Over time, as his fortunes improved, he'd become aware that women looked on him as a prize worth winning. His ability to trust was so eroded, however, he hadn't been willing to commit to anything serious. He didn't want to set himself up for another gross betrayal. Besides, he hadn't met anyone he couldn't stop thinking about.

Until Oriel.

It had been two months since he'd seen her, and he'd thought of her constantly, checking his phone like an adolescent hoping for a "like."

Surely she would have had a sign by now if the baby was his? He cautioned himself not to get caught up in a sense of duty toward her, but uneasily recognized he wouldn't cut all ties if it wasn't his. He had delivered the shock of her life. She was in a vulnerable state and could be even more so, depending on what this test told them. He couldn't wish her a nice life and go back to his own.

Damn it, why were there so many brands? He scanned the array of boxes, brain nearly exploding at the advertising flashing that promised "results in one minute" and "estimated weeks." He grabbed the two priciest ones and half expected her to be gone when he returned.

She had changed into plaid pajama pants and a T-shirt, washed off her makeup, removed her earrings, and gathered her hair into a low ponytail. She was as fresh-faced as when he'd met her that morning in Milan, except far more somber.

The soup had arrived. It sat untouched and covered on the tray on the small table.

She eyed the bag choked by his fist.

"Listen." He was too restless to sit. "Whether it's mine or not—"

"Of course it would be yours," she snapped. "Don't be rude!"

A sharp wave hit him at that declaration, one that winded him so thoroughly, it took him a second to find his voice again. A smart man would be cautious about taking her word for it, but a very primitive part of him was already aligning with this news, accepting it as truth.

He made himself say, "I thought you would have had some sign by now if that was a possibility?"

"I have really low body fat. I never have regular periods," she said stiffly, then pinched the bridge of her nose. "I've been feeling run-down, though. I threw up a few times. I thought it was a bug from travel. I've been exhausted for weeks, but I've been working nonstop. I thought it was burnout."

"I see." That sounded plausible. "Well, I'm here. No matter what." He spoke before he'd fully contemplated all that might entail, but he couldn't turn his back on her, not if he was responsible for what she was going through.

He held out the bag.

"I don't have to go yet," she said sullenly and looked out the window.

"Oh." He set the bag on the bed. "Should we watch TV while we eat?"

"Do whatever you want."

He lifted the cover off the soup, hoping the aroma

of leeks and potatoes and fresh rolls would tempt her, but she didn't even look at him.

He replaced the cover. "Do you want an apology?"

"For what? Producing, single-handedly, the absolute most stressful hours of my life? For completely overturning everything I thought I knew about myself while potentially wreaking havoc on my future?"

Vijay had had a few weeks to digest the news of her parentage and it was purely incidental to his own life, not rooted in his foundation. He was reeling under the idea that he might become a father, but he wouldn't let that sink in until he knew for sure she was pregnant and intended to keep it. For her, this meant her *body* would be taken over. He couldn't make assumptions about how she would proceed.

What remained constant through all of this, however, was his fascination with this woman. He was trying to keep his head and think about facts and next steps, but learning about her birth family had only meant something to him because it was about *her*. He was angry with himself that he hadn't handled this better.

"You have every right to be angry. And scared."

The corners of her mouth went down. "I have to go *so bad*." She looked to the bathroom. "But I'm afraid of what I'll find out. Then it will be real."

He couldn't stand it. He closed in on her, moving slowly so she had plenty of time to rebuff him, but he didn't know how else to express the conflicting emotions gripping him, the remorse and concern.

When he gathered her in, she shuddered and slid her arms around his waist, tucking her nose into the nook of his neck.

It was surprisingly powerful to hold her again, to feel this sense of interlocking his life with hers. Her scent filled his head and her breasts pressed his chest and her hair tickled his chin. He wanted to press his lips to her skin, but made himself speak against her hair.

"What *we* find out," he managed to say. He was taking her word for it that he was the only possible father, but he wanted to believe it, which was its own sort of terrifying. It wasn't just a latent desire to be a father, either. He wanted to be the father of *her* child.

And no matter what was going on in his head, it must be a thousand times worse for her. He knew that because she was trembling.

"You're not alone." He rubbed her back reassuringly. "I'm here."

She nodded and withdrew, biting her lip as she picked up the bag and moved to the bathroom.

Her silver gown was hanging on the door. She unhooked the hanger from the edge and threw the whole thing toward the bed, where it slithered to the floor. She didn't seem to care and closed the door behind her.

Vijay hung the gown on the curtain rod, then took her place staring at all those mindless people going on with their mindless lives around the pool. Didn't they know that life-altering discoveries were being made right now?

He reminded himself to breathe.

This was too much.

Oriel shakily did her thing, then set the test on the empty box on the back of the toilet without looking at the result. She stared into her ghoulish reflection as she washed her hands, fighting back a hysterical cackle. Her birth mother was a Bollywood icon? Her one-night lover was an undercover DNA thief? Her career was about to be derailed by an unplanned pregnancy?

Non. She might have been able to handle one or two of those things, but not all of them. Not all at once. It was too much. Way too much. Her vision was fading at the edges, she was working so hard to keep from breaking down.

Especially because, deep inside herself, she knew what she wanted that test to say, and it went against everything she had ever told herself. She had long ago decided that when she was ready for children, she would adopt. She understood how important it was to offer a good home to a child who needed one, and she had a lot of love to give as well as many advantages.

A man had not been a necessary part of that picture, deliberately. Of course, she had always hoped to find someone who would make a life and family with her, but her mother was an icon who had molded the life she wanted rather than waiting around hoping for it to manifest on its own. Seeing how Estelle had managed to have it all—career, marriage, family—had made Oriel open to the idea of having children on her own timeline, by herself, without waiting for a committed relationship if that was what felt right when the time came.

Pinning her future on a man was very last century, yet here she was, secretly hoping that test would tie her to Vijay forever. He didn't even want her! Not the way she longed to be wanted and loved. He might be nice enough to give her a hug when she was falling apart, but he'd also gone behind her back and *he hadn't called.*

As she turned off the taps, she heard a knock at the door. "Can I come in?"

"I haven't looked at it," she said flatly.

He came in uninvited.

She really should learn to lock him out of rooms she was in.

She ought to bash him in the chest and make him leave her alone, but that was the problem. She was feeling very, very alone right now. Who could she explain this to? Her agent? Her parents? She had cousins and friends, but they were scattered all over, and no one had any shared perspective. They would say the wrong things. You found your birth mother? Wonderful! But it wasn't. Her birth mother was already gone. You're pregnant? Exciting! But no. It meant the career that was finally taking off would fizzle.

You were treated badly by a man? Tell him to go to hell.

She couldn't. Because rather than lean around her to see the result, rather than take her by the shoulders and babble some unhelpful platitude, Vijay stood before her, quiet and calm, as though whatever happened next couldn't shake him. He was solid and demanded nothing. He was here for her, and that meant the world.

"Why didn't you want Jalil to date your sister?" she asked.

His brows went up at what must have sounded like a random question, but she'd been wondering ever since he'd mentioned it in Milan. Plus, she was putting off facing whatever that test was going to tell her.

What if she *wasn't* pregnant? Would she announce she hated him and send him on his way? She doubted she could do that, and that was the most disturbing discovery of all.

"Jalil is much older than Kiran. I thought he must be showing interest in her because of her youth or the money we stood to make in the acquisition."

"A nurse or a purse," Oriel murmured. "That's what one of my mother's friends says older men are looking for when they date younger women. I kept thinking of that when I was with Duke. That I was resuscitating his career for him. Administering oxygen so I could gain something for myself. I felt like a fame whore."

"Oof. Is this where the self-bashers meet? Because I feel like an ass for not believing my sister possesses sound judgment and knows her own heart. I interfered in her life and have overturned yours, all out of an arrogant belief that I know best."

She gave him a chiding look, but appreciated his acknowledging how much he had tripped her up. She appreciated his humor, too. She had liked that about him from the first.

"I can't tell Jalil anything about my birth mother," she pointed out. "The information I had was wrong."

"I think he just wants to know that a part of his sister lives on. I wouldn't want to be in his shoes, but if I was, I can imagine how much it would comfort me to discover Kiran had a child."

Oriel felt her mouth twisting at his sharing such a personal detail. She looked at her reflection—that remnant of a woman who was gone.

She noted the anxiety around her eyes, the lack of color in her lips. She had always known she was the result of an unplanned pregnancy, but she suddenly felt deep affinity for that mysterious person who had given birth to her. This was how Lakshmi must have felt. Overwhelmed. Frightened. Head pounding with the question, *What do I do*?

She couldn't imagine how much more difficult this would be if Vijay or someone else were pushing her around, telling her what to do. The way it was sounding, Lakshmi might have had to fight just to give birth to her.

A ferocity rose in her, an instinctual, angry determination that arrived in her like a gleaming light of truth.

"If I'm pregnant, I'm keeping the baby." Her eyes grew damp. It felt good to acknowledge that, even though it turned her crystal-clear future into a blurred vision through a fogged glass.

She looked straight at Vijay, letting him see that she would never be swayed on this.

He nodded thoughtfully, while his eyes narrowed with intensity.

"And if you're pregnant…it's definitely mine."

The way he said it made her heart lurch unsteadily in her chest. She wanted to set her chin with indignation, but it didn't sound as though he was questioning her. At the same time, she realized this was her chance to firmly eject him from her life if she wanted to.

She couldn't.

She swallowed the hot constriction in her throat. "Today I learned that everything I thought I knew about my birth parents was a lie. I wouldn't do that to my own child. You are definitely the father."

"Then, if you're pregnant—" he spoke with steady resolve "—I'll propose."

The impact of that was so monumental, her ears rang. Her chest felt as though it was pierced by a stinging arrow.

"You don't owe me anything." *Us.*

"I owe any child I make everything I am capable of providing."

Not about her, then. She realized how intently

they'd been staring into each other's eyes when she dropped her gaze. A giant brick seemed to settle between her lungs.

"I'll refuse," she warned through her tight throat. "I'm still angry with you. I don't trust you."

"Trust is difficult for me, too." His mouth twisted. "But this isn't about us, is it?"

"I don't know," she said, voice nearly nonexistent. "Maybe we're arguing over nothing." They weren't. Her intuition told her exactly what that test would say.

"Shall we see?"

Biting her lip, she nodded jerkily.

When she didn't turn to retrieve it, he crowded close. One of his arms went around her waist to steady her as he leaned past her.

She tensed, ears straining. She felt the jolt that went through him. He sucked in a breath and his chest expanded.

A shower of sparkling lights filled her vision. She closed her fists into his shirt, afraid she was going to faint.

He made a small space between them and showed her the stick. She had to blink and blink to see its bright blue, unmistakable cross that indicated a positive. In a voice husked with reverence, Vijay said, "We're having a baby."

CHAPTER SIX

ORIEL'S PHONE BEGAN emanating soft harp strings that gradually increased in volume.

As Vijay reached across her to turn it off, she reached for it herself.

She must have still been mostly asleep, because as their hands bumped and their bodies shifted against one another's, a startled gasp tore out of her throat. She sat up in a tangle of blankets, hair spilling across her face. She impatiently shoved it out of her eyes.

As she stared at him, recognition arrived with comprehension and memory. She sagged and pulled her knees up to hug them, giving a little choke of helplessness.

The angels in her phone grew more insistent. She grabbed it and stabbed to silence it.

"What's the alarm for?" His voice sounded like a garbage disposal. He cleared his throat.

"I'm flying home to spend the rest of the week with my parents. I told you that."

"That's your vacation? Do you have a flight booked?" He rolled toward the nightstand on his side, picking up his own phone, but ignored the notifications.

"Yes." She fell back onto her pillow and flicked through her messages.

His eyes were so gritty with lack of sleep, he could barely see his screen.

Last night, they'd eaten and she'd gone to bed while he had stood at the window, trying to assimilate the fact he was becoming a father. He might not trust easily, but after her indignant declaration about learning her birth history was a lie, he believed her about that much.

Family was an extremely complex knot of emotions for him. He had grieved the loss of his parents and grandmother with the support of his extended family. Then he lost his parents again when he realized what they'd been covering up. The people he had thought he knew had never existed. When he exposed that, he was called an ungrateful traitor and worse. The loving safety net he'd believed would always be there for him had been yanked like a rug. None of those relations would take his calls, and he was still angry and hurt enough that he wouldn't pick up the phone, either.

Only Kiran had stood by him, and he would give his life to protect her. He'd gotten used to thinking she was all he would ever have.

Now he had this nascent, fragile idea of a person beginning to take up space in his heart. There was no question in him that he would claim his child with every part of himself and ensure his child's life was intrinsically interwoven with his own.

So that meant doing the same with Oriel.

She was a far more complicated person to weave into his life. He still wanted her physically. Desire for her was simmering beneath all his best efforts to ignore it. He recalled her as an amusing, interesting companion over dinner, but real life was not a few hours of casual conversation. Real life was *real*. He knew very little about the real Oriel Cuvier.

He had thought he did. When she hadn't called, he had convinced himself she was too stuck-up to reach out to a blue-collar boy toy.

Beneath her animosity and shock about her birth parents and the baby news, she was angry with him, though. Hurt. Because she thought he'd deliberately given her the wrong number. Because she thought he had only come to her room for a toothbrush, not *her*.

As he'd stood at the window wondering if it was time for him to quit being so damned suspicious of everyone around him, he'd heard her sniffle and realized she was giving in to the volume of emotions drowning her. He had crawled into bed fully dressed and curled himself around her.

She'd cried herself to sleep, and maybe he had dozed. Mostly he'd stared into the darkness, working through the thousand paths forward, trying to find the best one. His entire life needed to be reshaped around her and their child. They had a lot of decisions to make.

"Are you flying into Tours?" he asked her, recalling where her parents' home was located. "What time does your flight leave?"

"Nine thirty."

"Nine thirty-eight?" It was the only one aside from another in the late afternoon. "It's not giving me a seat selection. I don't think we'll be able to sit together." He booked it anyway.

"I can't take you home with me." She sat up. "What do expect? That you'll just sleep with me in my old bedroom?" She gave their shared blankets a disdainful look.

"If there's no room in your parents' *chateau*…" He wondered how she would react when he told her where *he* came from. "Then I'm sure I'll be able to find something online."

"I'm not being a snob," she said impatiently. "I'm saying I don't know what to tell them. Who am I supposed to say you are?"

"Your fiancé?" he suggested pleasantly.

"Oh, was I asleep when you proposed? I didn't hear it."

"Because you told me you would refuse." He sat up and swung his legs off his side of the bed, not wanting her to see that her rebuff had landed and left a bruise. "I'm saving my breath until I've answered a few questions for myself."

"Such as?" She dropped her feet off her side of the mattress, but twisted to look at him.

He looked over his shoulder at her. "You travel for work and I'm president of the Asia division. How will we address that? Where would we call home?"

She held his gaze. Swallowed. Then she gave him her back again. "You're right. I don't want to talk about it. I'm planning to tell my parents about…" Her voice grew muffled as she looked down and spoke to her lap. "About my birth mother. But that's all. For now."

Did it sting that she didn't want to tell her parents she was pregnant with his baby? Yes, but he accepted that the news about her birth family was delicate enough.

"I haven't told Jalil that I've spoken to you." They were still sitting back to back with the width of the mattress between them. "If you're not ready to speak to him, I'll tell him you need time to break it to your parents. He'll understand. I can say your work schedule is very demanding, and you'll be in touch when you have a break."

She gave a humorless choke of laughter. "I'll have to tell my agent that I'm pregnant. Once I do that, I anticipate my work schedule will become much less demanding *very* quickly."

"Oriel." He twisted to set his hand in the middle of the mattress. "I—"

"Don't say you're sorry." She rose abruptly. "I know I'm sounding bitchy. I'm not blaming you. The timing could definitely be better, but I'm not sorry I'm pregnant."

Nor was he, which was a very strange realization to absorb.

He rose and opened the curtains, letting in a blast of morning sunlight that made him wince.

When he turned to look at her, she was staring at him. She stood in bare feet and rumpled pajamas with unbrushed hair. Her face was naked, her brow crinkled.

He decided this was how he liked her best, even though she was so lacking in defenses, it made his chest tighten.

"Were you planning to have kids at some point?"

She gave a confused shrug. "My career hasn't left a lot of room for thinking about starting a family. When I did, I didn't worry too much about whether my fertile years were passing me by. I've always assumed I would adopt because I was adopted."

She chewed her lip, and her brow wrinkled even harder as she continued. "I've always felt loved by all my family, but there's no ignoring the fact that everyone looks and sounds like at least one other person. They have odd quirks that mark them as related. I tried not to let it bother me that I didn't have that because it couldn't be changed, but I've always had this sense of…missing out. Or…missing someone?" Her mouth trembled, and she firmed her lips.

The sun caught on the dampness in her lashes, making his lungs burn.

"I'm so sorry I'll never meet Lakshmi. That's what I was crying about last night. I do want to meet Jalil, sooner than later. And I want to meet this baby." She set her hand on her belly. "I'm really excited to see…" Her smile wavered with emotion. "A little bit of myself?"

His heart caved in. He moved around the bed, reaching for her.

She threw her hand up to hold him off. "I'm still angry with you."

"Fair." He caught her hand and used it to reel her closer. "But know that I feel the same. That baby is a part of me, and I can't imagine not being in our child's life every day."

Her gaze searched his, and the question was on his lips. *Will you marry me?* Even the bright sunshine and dancing dust motes became too much to have between them. He drew her closer, softly crashing her curves into his hardening body.

He wanted to kiss her. Hell, he wanted to take her to bed and reestablish the connection they had shared in Milan. Her lashes fluttered, and her mouth trembled. Her grip tightened on his fingers where their hands were clasped.

He had been waiting for this, the warmth of her, the scent in her hair, the feel of her as he drew her closer. He tipped his head and started to lower his mouth across her parted lips—

"I don't think that's a good idea." She jerked back and pulled herself free of him.

The chill of her absence was an abrupt bucket of ice water splashing over him. He pushed his hands into his pockets, hoping to disguise that he was aroused.

"I did try to text." She was hugging herself again. "But you didn't. You've only ever sought me out for…investigative purposes."

"That's not true." If she only knew how obsessed he'd been all these weeks. "I had dinner with you because I wanted to. I shouldn't have come to your room without telling you everything, but I couldn't stay away. That's the truth, Oriel." He ran his hand through his hair, agitated at being forced to reveal himself this way. "When you didn't get in touch after, I accepted that you didn't want to pursue anything beyond what we'd agreed to. But once Jalil's theory panned out, I had to see you again. I wanted to see if we still react to each other like this. And we do."

Lust was a churning furnace within him, waiting to explode at the first breath of oxygen she blew across it.

She hugged herself and eyed him warily.

"Wanting to kiss you and make love to you isn't an *idea*," he said. "It's attraction. I wanted to see you again. Jalil's news gave me the excuse. Now we've learned we're having a baby, and our lives are going to be linked forever. I can understand if you're worried sex will cloud things or you simply don't feel up to it, but seducing you isn't some master plan on my part. I'm reacting to being near you, same as you are to me."

"That's exactly what I'm doing—reacting! I can't keep a lucid thought in my head or figure out what comes next. My hormones are saying, 'Have sex. Then you don't have to think at all.' That's not going to solve anything."

"I don't know," he drawled. "My hormones would

love a sidebar with yours. Maybe we should give it to them, see what they accomplish."

"Pfft." She dissolved into the prettiest laughter he'd ever heard. "Nice try."

He shrugged. "Worth a shot."

The air crackled with awareness and possibility and the panting breath of a wolf circling his mate. Her eyes widened, and she licked her lips. He started to close in on her, but her phone released a more aggressive sound of church bells.

"I always set two, in case I sleep through one," she said, moving to silence it. "And I can't miss this flight. My parents are expecting me." She glanced warily at him.

"I'm coming with you," he reminded her. "We have a lot to talk about."

She started to say something, but her gaze focused with annoyance over his shoulder, and she tsked. "I forgot the garment bag for this on the yacht."

She circled around him to ruffle the gown he'd left hanging from the curtain rod.

Vijay ran his tongue over his teeth.

"I'll call the concierge. I'm sure they can send something up." He moved to pick up the hotel phone, then paused. He had to know. "*Was* it a gift from Duke?"

"Maman." She splayed the skirt to look for flaws. "For their anniversary party. She'll be annoyed that I haven't been caring for it properly. It will have to be cleaned and steamed. Repaired." She touched a loose thread at the hem. "You can have my bed at the chateau, because I'll be in the doghouse."

He snorted, but her smile faded. She seemed to remember that a less than perfect gown was the least of the things that could potentially upset her mother.

He wanted to tell her it would be okay, but he didn't know that. All he knew was that she'd just conceded to his going to Tours with her. That was enough for now.

He called down for a garment bag and ordered breakfast at the same time.

Oriel didn't protest Vijay coming home with her. He was the father of her unborn baby. Whether she married him or not, he ought to meet her parents.

They arrived to chaos. Caterers and decorators and workmen were overrunning the place, erecting marquee tents and unloading tables, chairs, linens and dishes.

Her mother would be in her element. It was the sort of orchestration she loved best. She was not only the center of attention—her rightful place—but she was director, producer, and critic, providing a swift review if a flower head sagged or a bulb on a string failed to light.

"When you said the gown was for your parents' anniversary party…" Vijay said as they climbed from the car at the bottom of the steps.

"Um, yes. It's tonight." She grimaced as she realized she hadn't exactly prepared him. "It's just an intimate affair with three hundred of Maman's closest friends and colleagues. I did mention that she is beloved? The spare room in my suite please, Tauseef," Oriel directed as her mother's chauffeur retrieved their luggage.

Vijay lifted a brow at her. She lifted a shoulder at him. She was angry and wary of trusting him again, but she kept thinking about him saying, *I shouldn't have come to your room without telling you everything, but I couldn't stay away.*

She was equally compelled to keep him near. The way he'd held her last night had been deeply comforting. He was right that they had a lot to talk about, and she couldn't help wondering if they might have something beyond what looked on the surface to be a complete disaster.

Maybe she was kidding herself, but there was only one way to find out.

She led him into the house, where it was easy enough to locate her mother. She was nearly always in the music salon even when she wasn't singing.

They went through the oval-shaped foyer with its curved staircase and domed ceiling, then passed the large sitting room with its grand fireplace and row of arched windows that looked onto the grounds. Abundant furniture was arranged in pockets for her parents' frequent houseguests and evening soirees. On their other side, they passed the formal dining room with its long table and westward-facing windows that caught the sunset on the pond, and finally arrived at the octagonal-shaped room where her mother spent most of her time.

The music salon was no less exquisitely built than the rest of the modern chateau, but it was kept free of carpets and pollen and other dust-producers so as to preserve Madame's voice. Like her bedroom, the windows were triple-paned and the humidity carefully monitored and controlled. The grand piano was played every day while she exercised her vocal cords.

Today Estelle was surrounded by her entourage of assistants, agents, and designers along with some of Oriel's favorite aunties and cousins.

"Chou. At last." Estelle came forward to embrace Oriel, kissing each of her cheeks.

Madame Estelle was only five and a half feet tall, but she was such an imposing presence she seemed to be at least six and a half. Her hair was wrapped in a silk turban unless she was performing or making an appearance. Today, she wore one of her colorful caftans in bright yellow and magenta. It made her dark brown skin glow. She had been born with an assertive personality and tremendous operatic talent. As her voice had developed and her status rose, she had become a powerhouse in the entertainment business and a diva everywhere else.

Introductions were made, and Oriel gave and accepted all the kisses. Her mother eyed Vijay with curiosity. "A fellow model?"

"No," he dismissed with a self-conscious twitch of his mouth. "It's flattering you think I could be, but I'm in security technology."

"Vijay is the President of TecSec's Asia division," Oriel provided.

"Oh? We use them ourselves. I imagine you have many secrets about your private clients that you will refuse to let me worm out of you, but I shall enjoy the challenge of trying. I'm so glad you brought someone interesting." Estelle tapped Oriel's arm. "I feared you would bring that tired actor. I didn't know much about him, but what I did know made me certain I didn't need to know more."

Madame Estelle could get away with speaking her mind like that. Oriel would have chuckled along with everyone else, but she was too anxious over what she had to reveal.

"Where is Papa?" she asked.

"In his citadel, taking refuge from the chaos. Go along and say hello. Come down to visit after you've settled in."

"Will you come with me, please? There's something I need to discuss with you both."

"Cherie, I have so much to do, and our darling family is here." She waved at all the faces that had grown avid with curiosity. "You'll be here all week. Can it wait?"

"It can't." Oriel smiled an apology, but let her mother see her firmness.

Estelle gave Vijay another sidelong look. "Are you here in a professional capacity, Monsieur Sahir?"

"I'll let Oriel explain," he said with equanimity as he fell into step alongside her down the hall.

Moments later, they entered the library where

Oriel's father, Arnaud, wrote his papers and studied his historical research.

Arnaud was the perfect foil for Estelle. He was a quiet, patient man who could sit for hours in dressing rooms and concert halls or amid the babble of creative people who were his wife's constant companions. If he wasn't actively reading, he held a book with his finger notched between the pages. He had absolutely no desire for a spotlight, but was sincere and effusive in his praise of his wife for earning her place in hers.

Oriel had always felt completely loved and supported by him, but also as though she was a creature he didn't quite understand. Today, her sense of being an alien was stronger than ever. She worried they would both feel slighted by what she was about to tell them.

Her hands were so clammy, her father frowned with concern when he took them. He kissed both her cheeks, then shook Vijay's hand, studying him enquiringly as Oriel nervously closed the doors.

"Are we to have an engagement announcement at our anniversary?" Estelle asked with obvious delight as she perched herself on the arm of her husband's chair. "There would be some lovely symmetry to that."

"No, Maman." Oriel glanced at Vijay, silently begging him to say nothing about the baby.

He lowered himself to sit beside her on the sofa, and she took strength from his unflinching gaze and supportive silence.

"Vijay is an envoy from my birth family."

Estelle was rarely taken aback. Her breath went in as though she was doing her most aggressive breathing exercises. She rose with quiet grace and moved to her husband's sideboard, where she poured brandy with heavy liquid gurgles.

Oriel waited until her mother had handed out all the glasses and had perched on the chair again, taking Arnaud's hand in her own.

Oriel set her own drink aside and kept to the facts, skipping over absconded toothbrushes and a dinner-turned-dalliance. She simply relayed what Vijay had told her about Lakshmi, and that Jalil wished to meet her.

"I don't understand," Estelle said. "The clinic told us Oriel's birth parents were from Romania."

"I can only presume that was a red herring meant to protect Lakshmi's identity," Vijay said. "We've been trying to learn more about the clinic itself, but it closed two decades ago."

"Are you concerned there was impropriety? They came highly recommended. The lawyer who handled our side of the paperwork will be here tonight. He's above reproach," her mother insisted. "We had our name registered with several organizations at the time. This clinic was the first to contact us. They said the young woman liked our profile. We weren't attempting anything shady."

"I'm not suggesting you were. We may never know the complete truth about how Lakshmi came to give Oriel up. The important thing is that nothing we do learn could change the fact that you and Oriel are a family." Vijay looked at Oriel as he spoke, reinforcing that he wasn't here to take anything away from anyone. "Jalil has concerns the manager may have behaved unethically, though. If he did, he would like to see justice served."

"Of course." Estelle touched her throat. "Oriel isn't in any danger, is she?"

"Not to my knowledge, but if and when this news becomes public, you should expect a great deal of attention." Vijay sent Oriel a grimace of apology. "There is one other detail I haven't made clear to you. Jalil regards Lakshmi's estate as rightfully belonging to her child. In euros, it's worth over a hundred million."

"What? Non!" Oriel would have leaped to her feet, but her bones dissolved. "Please stop giving me these shocks. I'll need defibrillator paddles!"

He chuckled and reached across to squeeze her hand. "Whether you accept it or not is between you and Jalil. I'm telling you so you can plan security. You'll need it." He glanced at her parents. "I suggest you keep this news to yourselves until you have a full contingent of bodyguards in place, especially for the initial excitement. If you don't mind, I'll introduce myself to your security team while I'm here, purely as a courtesy."

"Of course." Arnaud nodded.

"Très bien." Estelle rose from the arm of the chair in her take-charge way. "We will discuss details tomorrow, but tonight the show goes on." Her glance

bounced off where Vijay still had his hand over Oriel's. "We don't want you to *look* like a bodyguard, Monsieur Sahir. Did you bring a tuxedo? Our party is white tie. Oriel, Max is in the pool house if you need assistance." She clapped her hands. "Four hours to curtain, my dears."

"Max" was Madame Estelle's personal designer. He tailored the entire family and had a full team offering an array of spa services from the cabanas around the pool.

Vijay was led there by the head of security after he and Oriel had made their rounds together.

Oriel had retired to her room by then, and Vijay hoped she was resting. He had thought her parents had taken the news as well as possible, but she'd seemed very withdrawn after.

He was concerned about her, but after walking the estate and getting a true sense of her family's net worth, he was concerned about *them*.

Back when he'd proposed to Wisa, he'd thought they were on the same level of wealth and privilege. As it turned out, his family's wealth had been illgotten. The fallout of discovering that had contributed to their extremely ugly breakup.

Vijay had had to start over. He was extremely comfortable now, but even though he was evolved enough not to feel threatened by the idea of a woman making more money than he did, he couldn't help being aware he would never catch up to Oriel if she stood to inherit all of this *and* all of Lakshmi's wealth. It shouldn't matter in a relationship, but it would always have the potential to.

Despite that, he kept coming around to their marriage being inevitable. He wasn't so rich in family that he could afford to let his own child be raised away from him. Oriel seemed equally devoted to being a full-time parent. That meant at least living together.

He wanted marriage, though, and not for entirely logical reasons. Wisa had proved to him that a ring didn't ensure fidelity, but the vows and formality of marriage were something *he* would take seriously. He wanted that stability for their child, but he wanted it for himself, too. And he couldn't help thinking that making those promises to each other would go a lot further in earning each other's trust than keeping their options open.

Could they make a marriage work, though? The differences in their backgrounds became even more obvious as Max asked him to remove the tuxedo he'd just tried on so it could be altered on the spot.

While he waited, Vijay's beard was sculpted and his hair trimmed. He was given a manicure for the first time in his life, even though he was also given gloves to wear. His shirt required cuff links, and gold ones appeared. The points of his white vest were a precise quarter-inch beneath the edge of his split-tailed jacket. The jacket's lapels matched the satin stripe down his trouser seams. New shoes in his size fit perfectly over his fresh silk socks. His bow tie was snow white.

Vijay might have felt overdressed and pretentious, maybe even resentful of being forced to fit in, if he hadn't looked so damned good.

He was directed to join the flock of penguins in the drawing room, where he noted that not all of the tuxedo-wearers were men. Vijay wasn't sure what they were waiting for, but they were all offered a signature cocktail with cognac lemon from sugar-rimmed glasses. Arnaud introduced Vijay to everyone and explained how each person was related to Oriel.

Vijay wasn't intimidated by titles or political power, but this level of society underscored even more how different he and Oriel were. They could negotiate how and where they would live, but at some point he would have to tell her about his father. How would she react to that?

"Monsieur," the butler said to Arnaud. "If you would like to assemble your guests in the front hall, the rest of the family will descend."

Vijay moved with the group into the entranceway.

Madame Estelle certainly enjoyed her pageantry. A trio of strings began to play as a name was announced. A woman floated down in an evening gown of peacock blue. She was met at the bottom by a man who brought her to a spot near the door, where they would form the head of the procession out to the marquee.

Cars were bumper to bumper on the drive. Guests had been queuing up on the red carpet for nearly an hour.

Vijay politely added his glove-muted applause for each person who came down in their glamorous and sophisticated evening wear, enjoying the drama of it.

"Mademoiselle Oriel Cuvier," the butler called.

His heart unexpectedly rose into his throat as he waited for her to appear.

He'd already seen her in the gown. The sight of her shouldn't have affected him, but she was entirely too beautiful for him not to feel his breath punched right out of him as she moved into the light at the top of the stairs.

Her hair was up again, but she wore a tiara that cast sparks of light between her piles of curls. Her earrings were matched by a stunning necklace that dripped ice down her cleavage. Her elbow-length gloves were silver to match her gown, and she wore a cuff of diamonds over her left wrist.

He had not appreciated her ability to command attention purely by the way she moved, but the gown and jewels all became secondary to the enigmatic mystique she projected as she descended, seemingly oblivious to everyone watching her.

Her eyes found him, though. Her gaze beckoned him to the bottom of the stairs. The smoldering sensuality in her expression stoked a fire in him. When he offered his arm, she bestowed a smile on him that sent a rush of pride through him. Pride that she found him pleasing. Pride that he was the escort for this stunning woman whose touch on his arm became a hot ember in his chest.

They moved into their place in the procession and turned as her mother was announced.

"Thirtieth anniversary is pearl," Oriel whispered.

Madame appeared in a gown covered in luminescent seed pearls. It rustled softly as she came to a halt at the top of the stairs and waited for the clapping to subside.

The music changed, and she began to sing. Her voice climbed and fell with deep emotion, filling the high-ceilinged space with every octave of love imaginable as she slowly made her way down.

Vijay didn't understand a word, but he felt his own heart rising and wrenching. The way Estelle never removed her eyes from her husband told him she meant every syllable. It was magnificent.

After his broken engagement, Vijay had convinced himself love was a sentiment sold by greeting cards and Bollywood musicals, but as he watched Arnaud cross to the bottom of the stairs and hold up his hand for his wife, with his face flushed and his eyes aglow, there was no denying the pair shared something beautiful and precious. It made Vijay feel small to be so cynical when, for some, love was absolutely real.

As the song ended and the final notes faded, Arnaud said, *"Mon coeur."*

The pair kissed, and everyone applauded once more.

Oriel's expression was gleaming with fierce love for them, but Vijay thought he glimpsed envy there, too. When her naked gaze lifted to his, his heart lurched. He read her question plain as day.

She wanted what her parents had.

He needed to be completely honest with her from here on out. He'd been burned deeply by love, not just by his fiancée's infidelity, but also by his own father's betrayal. He didn't trust lightly anymore and wouldn't give up his heart easily to anyone.

When she looked at him like that, however, he wanted to promise her the world.

CHAPTER SEVEN

"WOULD YOU LIKE to dance?"

Oriel was spellbound by the romance of the evening. The marquee was strung with fairy lights, the air laden with the scent of roses and jasmine. A twenty-piece orchestra played between courses and speeches. Several songs and recitations had been performed by close friends of the celebrating couple. She herself had given a final, heartfelt toast to her parents, and her mother had left everyone in tears with one more song that had earned her a standing ovation.

Now Estelle and Arnaud, had started the dancing and Vijay was standing over her, offering his gloved hand.

She was losing her mind over how sexy he was, and it had nothing to do with the tuxedo. It was all him. His sensual mouth and half-lidded eyes were pure seduction, his air of alert watchfulness and quiet command delicious.

She almost wished things had gone worse with her parents. Then she could hate him and use her resentment to hold him off. As it was, she was falling under his spell as easily as she had that night in Milan. Had she learned nothing? He was a destroyer of worlds.

"You waltz?" Her heart tripped as she placed her hand in his and he helped her rise.

Of course he waltzed. He was a man of infinite capabilities, hidden depths and fascinating angles.

"I know the basics. Don't expect…that," he said with a wry look at her cousin, who had married her fellow champion and partner from the professional ballroom circuit. They were swirling around the floor with airy grace.

"We're a family of overachievers." Oriel swooned as he took her in steady arms and confidently led her into the steps. "That's why it was so hard to find my niche and why I still feel only moderately successful." She was babbling out of nerves and felt like she had said too much when he frowned with perplexity.

"You seem pretty successful to me."

"Well, yes. I am. I mean, most women would kill for the opportunities I enjoy, but my work is based on genetic luck and tricks like attending high-profile premieres with attention-starved actors. It's not the same as rising through practice and mastering of craft."

"Your work is still a performance. You have to distill a mood down to a single snapshot. I saw you do it tonight when you came down the stairs. I was captivated."

"You don't have to build me up," she said with

discomfort. "Maman and I made our peace with our differences a long time ago. I'm just saying…this is a lot to live up to," she ended on a mumble.

"I was being sincere, but okay. How are things between you and your mother now? Is she upset by the news?"

"Unsettled. She came to my room earlier. We had a heart-to-heart." And enough tears they had had to use cool compresses after or risk looking like puffy-eyed newts at the ball. "She said she always knew this could happen, and she only wants whatever I want. She asked about you. She wanted to know if you were more than my sort of bodyguard."

"And you said?"

She didn't know! She had first been drawn to him because he had sparked a more intense attraction within her than she'd ever experienced before. Since then, he'd made her feel *all* the emotions in the most intense ways. She couldn't help but be wary of what more could come.

"I told her I'm trying to keep my distance since I have enough to worry about."

"Trying," he mused, mouth curving. "That sounds like you're having to work at it."

My hormones would love a sidebar with yours.

If her presence here for her parents' celebration hadn't been so important to her, she might have allowed them to fall into bed at the hotel. Vijay was an incredibly compelling man, confident and handsome and still capable of waking her senses with a glance. The fact he knew what she was going through and was actually facing her unplanned pregnancy *with* her made her gravitate to him even more.

She'd been starkly honest when she'd told him she was tempted to lose herself in the same wild excitement they'd shared in Milan so she didn't have to think about the more mundane and difficult details of how they would proceed. Maybe there was something very basic to her desire, too. Her body recognized he was the father of her child and yearned to pair-bond with him as a way of reinforcing their connection, ensuring he would look after both of them.

No matter what it was, she was breathless and dizzy as he steered her from the cloying scent of cigar smoke and gave her a small twirl as the song ended.

He caught her close. "How are you feeling? It's been a long day."

"I had a nap before I dressed." She was giddy from being in his arms, smiling even after he eased his hold and started to lead her off the floor. "I'm glad for the distraction of this party. Thank you for being my date. I know this is a lot."

"What I find most fascinating is that I have the feeling this sort of evening is not unusual for you." He nodded at the mime performing for a table.

"Not at all. Maman adores setting a stage and creating an experience. She began planning this two years ago, after Papa's sixtieth birthday."

"When I tell Kiran that tumblers served dessert *while it was on fire*, she will die."

Oriel laughed. "I can't wait to meet her. Will

she be on the call with Jalil tomorrow?" They had agreed they would call in the morning for a brief introduction.

Vijay's expression froze.

Her heart stopped. "No? You don't want me to meet her?"

"No, of course. I hadn't considered how much I have to tell her. I won't say anything about—" He dropped his gaze to her middle. "Not yet. But..."

"I know. It keeps hitting me at odd times, too." Aside from avoiding more than a sip of champagne when she toasted her parents, Oriel hadn't been letting herself think too much about the fact she was carrying his baby.

His hand came to her upper arm in a small caress. "Tell me if you need anything."

She nodded. He stood close enough that she could feel the warmth of his body. Her shoulder was still tingling from his touch, and his mouth was right there.

Seducing you isn't some master plan on my part.

Wasn't it, though?

His gaze touched her mouth, and his lips twitched. "Bodyguard, you said?"

"*You* said it. We all went along with it even though you were holding my hand."

"I was, wasn't I? I'm thinking about doing it again."

"Holding my hand?" She tried to suppress her grin, but her heart was soaring with excitement. Why? It was only hand-holding, for heaven's sake!

Even so, she gave him a coquettish bat of her lashes. "Perhaps while I accompany you on a patrol of the grounds?"

"I'm sure I'm overdue for that." As he let his knuckles brush against hers, he dipped his head to speak in her ear. "I know you dislike that awkward moment of wondering whether a man will kiss you, so I'll warn you now. I intend to."

Her skin tightened with anticipation, and she opened her fingers for the weave of his.

It was a chilly night, something she felt as soon as they were away from the marquee. The music faded and the stars opened above them.

They weren't the only ones seeking a moment of privacy. They passed two other couples tucked into shadows before they found a pocket among the hedges where the cool scent of cedar closed around them.

Oriel slid her arms over his hard shoulders and curled her hands behind his head, expecting the crash of his mouth onto hers.

He barely grazed her mouth with his own, running his lips across her jaw and blowing softly against her ear, making shivers rise up her arms and into her nape before he came back to lightly nibble on her bottom lip.

With a frustrated sob, she pressed herself tighter to him and slanted her mouth with invitation. He reacted by sealing them into the swirling darkness of a deep, passionate kiss, one that made them both groan in gratification.

His hands roamed her back and hips, pulling her tighter into the hardness behind his fly. When his tongue brushed hers, she sucked delicately. His whole body hardened and his fingers dug into her backside, holding her tight as he rocked her against his aroused flesh.

Oh, why be coy? She had known what she wanted in Milan, and she knew it just as clearly tonight. She dragged her head back.

"Let's go inside."

His nostrils flared. "For?"

"You need me to spell it out? I want to continue the affair we started. See where it might have gone."

His gaze was flinty, his caress on her jaw light. "An affair is something you can walk away from. We're beyond that."

She couldn't argue, not with his baby growing inside her, but lust had its talons dug into her. "You don't want to see what our hormones can accomplish?"

He snorted and said in a graveled voice, "I'm quite sure they can level a city." His mouth tightened. "You realize this is all I think about? I don't have much room left in my head for being noble. Be sure, Oriel."

"I am." From a physical standpoint, at least. She led him into a side entrance up to her rooms.

Her suite was a pair of bedrooms off a shared sitting room, all with tall windows overlooking the pond. The curtains were already drawn, the only light a stained-glass lamp casting red and blue streaks across the walls and ceiling.

"Have I told you that you are the most beautiful woman I have ever seen?" He leaned against the door as he locked it.

"Have I told you that you are the sexiest man I have ever seen?" With slow deliberation, she bit one finger of her glove and began to draw it off, making a show if it.

"Is that how we're playing?" He loosened his bow tie and opened one collar button. "Strip tease?"

"It seems a shame to waste the costumes. I was barely going to undress at all." She sent him her most beguiling look and came across to press the hand that was still gloved against his fly.

He looked down at her diamond bracelet, which flashed and sparkled. His breath hissed in, and his whole body went taut.

"I can definitely work with that," he said with a slow, wicked smile.

His gloved hand cupped her neck, and he ran his hot mouth into her throat. His other hand worked a finger beneath the neckline of her gown. The cool silk of his glove scraped erotically across her nipple, making tight golden wires shoot heat into her loins.

She fumbled at his fly and got her gloved hand into his pants. As she caressed and fondled, his teeth took hold of her bottom lip, and they stared into one another's eyes. His pupils were huge and glazed with feral passion right before he slid his arms around her and plundered her mouth with his own.

This was what she had wanted to feel again—*alive*. Connected. She was still angry at his subterfuge, but this incredible desire had pulled her toward him from the first, and it was still here. *He* was. Kissing her as though he would consume her. Wrapping his arms around her as though she was everything he needed in life.

She was so lost to the passion of their kiss, she didn't realize he had backed her to the bed until he tilted her onto it. She gasped and braced her hands on the mattress, but he was already lifting her gown, caressing her legs.

"The number of times I have thought about doing this again…" He went to his knees, and the heat of his mouth scorched the inside of her knee. He took soft, playful bites of her inner thigh, swirling his tongue against her skin until her legs trembled. Then the warmth of his mouth settled against the silk covering her most tender flesh. He began to lick around the edges of lace.

"Vijay," she moaned helplessly and sank onto her back in surrender.

He shifted the silk aside to anoint her until she was molten with need. She dove her fingers into his hair and arched, abandoning herself to the pleasure he bestowed, but he didn't take her over the edge.

When she was sobbing and tense and lifting into his caress, he rose and said, "Do you mind?" as he gently rolled her onto her stomach. "I just want to see how you look with the shoes and this icicle dress up around your waist—"

His voice faded into a guttural curse as she accepted the challenge and owned it. She planted her feet apart and braced her elbows on the bed, then arched her back to lift her bottom. She cast him a provocative look over her shoulder.

Did he think she didn't know how to use her sex appeal to achieve a desired result?

His breath was rattling unevenly as his hands moved over her buttocks and thighs, caressing everywhere but the place she ached most. He told her how sexy she was. How much he wanted her as he slowly, slowly drew her panties down her legs.

When he crouched to draw them free of her ankles, his teeth scraped the tendon at the back of her thigh where her leg met her cheek.

She shook in reaction, hands fisting in the blankets as she waited in agony while he caressed her calves and kissed the back of one knee, then stood. She heard the rustle of his pants as he freed himself.

"Do you want to roll over?" His voice was deep and far away, buried in layers of carnal hunger.

"No. Like this…"

"Naked?"

"Yes." She could hardly speak as his hot tip began to trace and slide, seeking, then pressing for entrance.

She was so wet and aroused, he entered her in one smooth, steady thrust that made them both groan with abandon. His hands splayed to brace her hips before he slid his palms up to her waist, exposing more of her.

"You're exquisite." His powerful thighs shifted hers apart a little more, feet planting firmly between hers. He took hold of her hip and shoulder and began to thrust with lazy power.

She pressed her face into the mattress, moaning unreservedly. It was base and hot and no one else had ever broken her down this way, pushing her past inhibition into a state of pure animalistic pleasure. No one could hold her on this pinnacle of acute near-climax for what felt like hours, so she was lost to all but the exquisite sensations rolling through her in waves.

Only him. Only him.

Then, just as she thought she would break from the agony of resisting satisfaction, his hand roamed to where they were joined. His long finger caressed across the swollen bud of her clitoris, strumming and sending her shooting past the limits of her control. She exploded, crying out at the sudden power of it.

He gave a final deep thrust and joined her with a ragged shout.

"We may not have thought this through." Vijay could hardly speak, let alone find the strength to shift his weight off her back. He grunted with profound loss as he pulled free of her and collapsed on the bed beside her, legs dangling off the mattress.

It had taken everything in him not to hammer into her the way he'd longed to. Somehow, that controlled, exquisite lovemaking had been even more intense and left him utterly shredded.

"I have nothing left to get undressed." Speaking was an effort.

"Same." She turned her head on the mattress to blink at him. Her eyelids were heavy with gratification, adding a layer of smugness to his satisfaction.

"Was I too rough?" He had managed to hold back until the very end, but he'd lost some control as they'd hit their peak. This woman completely dismantled him every single time. He'd known it in Milan and had known it when they stood outside, necking in the hedges. He'd known coming in here that she would pull him apart in ways that weren't comfortable, but he'd done it anyway.

That bothered him, yet here he was.

"I liked it." Her smile kept the erotic memory glowing between them like a golden light of promise. "But you're right. This won't be my most graceful moment." She stole his pocket square and asked, "Can you get my zip?"

He did, stealing a caress of her spine before she pushed up from the mattress. As she straightened, she let the gown fall to the floor in what was actually a very supple, unselfconscious display of glorious nudity before she disappeared into the bathroom.

With superhuman strength, he tucked himself back into his fly and rose to pick up her gown. He was still looking for the hanger when she appeared in a pink silk robe.

"That poor gown." She tutted. "*Never* tell my mother what it's been through."

"You think I'm going to tell your mother that I bent you over the bed and made love to you in it?"

She found the hanger and came across with it, offering him a lingering kiss as she took the gown. Her hair was still up, her jewelry on, her makeup smudged in the most libidinous way.

He could get used to this, he decided as he began to undress. The fog of sexual satisfaction was particularly delicious while watching her move around her personal space, seeing her in a way that very few others were allowed to.

She slid a knowing smile at him when she caught him admiring her. A hunger that wasn't purely sexual nestled in the pit of his gut. It was desire for all of her. Her thoughts, her laughter, her moments of doubt. He imagined her belly swelling and being at liberty to press his hand there anytime so he could feel their baby kick.

At some point she would go into labor, and that thought was enough to send a cold rush of protectiveness through him, one that propelled him across to still her hands from fiddling with the gown. He gathered her in and kissed her, holding her close, trying to convey the myriad emotions gripping him.

Her arms came up around his neck, and for long moments they were lost to lazy, sexy kisses. When they broke to catch their breath, her hands slid down to his vest.

"Careful," she said with an unsteady smile. Her gaze skittered from his as though she was as unsettled by the intensity of the moment as he was. "We'll wind up forgetting to get undressed again."

He stole a last fondle of her bottom through the silk of her robe and released her.

"Who do I return this to and how do I pay for borrowing it?" He unbuttoned his vest. "Max wouldn't say."

"Because I bought it for you."

Vijay bristled.

"Oh, don't look at me like that." Oriel began to remove her jewelry and set it in a crystal bowl on the dresser. "You didn't expect or particularly *want* to attend this party."

He'd managed to put aside their different backgrounds and enjoy the evening, but it came around hard enough to slap him now.

"I can afford my own tuxedo, Oriel." Aside from tonight, he had no use for one and had no doubt this one was priced at a premium, given this had been a last-minute alteration, but he wasn't a pauper. He'd recently inked his name onto a deal that gave him a lot more disposable income than he'd had when he had bought her a gourmet dinner in Milan.

"My father can afford his own Maserati and rarely drives," she said, "but my mother still bought him one for his birthday. Don't worry about it."

"They're married," he pointed out. "If you're buying me clothes, does that mean you intend to marry me?"

"You haven't asked, have you?" she shot back. "But consider this before you do." She held up a finger like a scolding schoolteacher. "The reason my parents chose to adopt me was that my mother values her career. She has always had to work very hard to balance her personal aspirations with being a wife and a parent. Papa has a decent income from his books and papers, but Maman is the one who can afford a custom-built house like this. Yet she is constantly judged for not being maternal enough. For emasculating her husband by earning more and holding the spotlight while he takes a supporting role and arranges his life around her touring schedule. If the shoe were on the other foot, no one would bat an eye."

"You're warning me I will have to play second fiddle to you and the riches you stand to inherit? I'm well aware, Oriel." His voice hardened along with every muscle in his body. All his sexual afterglow was gone.

"I'm saying that if you're already threatened by it, you should definitely save your breath on proposing, because I won't marry you if you expect me to apologize for who I am or what I have." She waved at their surroundings. "I'm proud of my mother for all she has accomplished. I won't reject this or her to appease your ego."

Vijay removed his cuff links and dropped them into the dish with her own jewelry. The sound was very loud inside their thick silence.

"Those were a gift, too," she said frostily. "I thought it would be a nice keepsake from a special night. Most people were very honored to be included, but apparently this evening isn't something you consider worth remembering. Good to know. Sleep in the other room." She turned her back and started into her bathroom.

"My father was corrupt," he bit out, loath to talk about it, but it had to be addressed. This fight wasn't about whether their lovemaking was memorable—it was imprinted on his soul never to be forgotten—or whether he would keep a pair of cuff links. He probably should have mentioned this blight in his history before he started talking about marriage. "I was complicit in his crimes."

"What?" Her jaw went slack.

"Unknowingly." He ran his hand into his hair. "But it went on way too long. I'm deeply ashamed, but it's something you should know about me, whether or not we marry, given we share a child."

She moved to lower herself onto a velvet stool and blinked somber eyes at him. "What happened?"

"I told you my parents died when I was in my teens."

"And that you raised Kiran, yes."

He nodded abruptly. "She was in the car when they died. She uses a wheelchair now, which I only tell you to help you understand how I could have been so oblivious to what was going on beneath my nose. After we lost our grandmother, we still had possession of the house we grew up in. Technically our aunt had care of us, but she had a family and a busy medical practice in Delhi. We stayed in our home with some staff. I was Kiran's de facto guardian. She still required surgeries and other therapies. We were grieving and trying to move forward with our lives, going to school and making what felt like a normal life. My father's construction business continued to run under his top managers. I met with them once or twice a year, but I didn't involve myself in it. I was grateful I didn't have to worry about money on top of everything else."

"You were a child," she said, as if that might excuse his ignorance.

"I was fifteen when I started meeting with them. I was twenty-two before I took a proper interest in how the company turned such a healthy profit." He still hated himself for trusting so blindly. "When I did, I realized our success was built on bribery and backroom deals. Intimidation, in some cases."

"Are you sure those weren't the tactics of the people who were left in charge after your father passed?"

"I'm sure. They were following the playbook he had created when he took over a handful of broken-down machines from his own father. He had been bribing officials to win contracts for roads and bridges from day one. Sometimes he failed to meet the building requirements. At one point, a bridge had collapsed and they'd paid to cover up their deliberate watering down of material. Thankfully, no one was injured or killed, but it was only a matter of time. The level of corruption was astonishing."

"What did you do?" Her eyes were wide with muted horror.

"I took the evidence to the police. Records and assets were seized, arrests made. They were lenient with me because I cooperated, but we lost the house, the business. Everything of value. It was social and financial suicide. All of my friends were connected to the relationships my father had built. To avoid going down with the ship, many turned on us and tried to smear our name. When that happened, even our family turned their backs on us, especially my father's side."

"Because you were trying to make reparations for a wrong that wasn't even your crime? Since when is integrity worse than living off ill-gotten gains?" Oriel asked crossly.

"Since it affected their own social standing and ability to keep their jobs. But thank you for that." He pushed his hands into his pants pockets. "Kiran was the only one who stood by my decision to come clean. Everyone else said I should have kept my mouth shut and wound it down quietly if I didn't like it. Instead we had death threats. That's why Kiran started our security system, to protect us. Many people tried to undermine our success with it, retaliating by suggesting I employed my father's methods to win the few installations we were hired to make. Our success has been achieved honestly," he stressed. "Killian, the owner of TecSec wouldn't have touched us with a ten-foot pole otherwise. So it's not ego that makes me reluctant to accept your gift, Oriel. It's my conscience. I need to earn what I have."

* * *

What a terrible betrayal. She couldn't fathom how hurtful it would have been for him and his sister to lose everything, including their friends and family, after suffering so much loss already.

"I'll have Max invoice you if it's important to you."

"It is."

She nodded, compulsively running the silky tail of her robe's belt between her fingers. "I won't take that money from Jalil. It's not mine—"

"Don't let my feelings color yours." Vijay moved to crouch before her. His big hand stilled her fidgeting fingers. "Whether you accept that fortune or not is between you and him. Just as what you do with this…" he lifted his gaze to the ceiling of the chateau "…and the rest of what you inherit from your parents is completely up to you. I don't expect you to renounce any of it. Just know that if we marry, people are going to suggest I came after you for your money. That will get under my skin sometimes, and now you know why. But I know what I'm worth. And it's not insubstantial."

Nothing about him was insubstantial. He would be a lot more easy to dismiss if he was.

"Okay, but I hope you won't think what you just told me, or the fact I will inherit all of this, has anything to do with my concerns about whether or not we marry. We barely know each other, Vijay. I always imagined that if I married, it would be because…" Why did it make her feel so gauche to admit it? "That I would be in love."

He didn't laugh. He accepted that with a nod of understanding and stood.

"Did you know that something like ninety percent of marriages in India are still arranged?" he asked. "The couples aren't usually strangers anymore, but they don't always know each other well. Even so, our divorce rate is really low. People wind up very content. Why don't we approach it that way? Tell me what you're looking for in marriage beyond love."

What else was there?

"I always thought love was the key," she said. "My parents have very different personalities, but they're in love, and that seems to be what makes their marriage work."

"I'm not going to promise you a life of love, or even that I'm capable of falling in love. But looking at your parents as an outsider, I see a couple who seem to have friendship, respect, affection. Loyalty. We could have those things."

It was a fair offer, but seemed like a pale knock-off version of the connection she really yearned for.

"What do you want?" she asked, playing her fingers into the space between his shirt buttons. "Don't say 'someone who cooks.' I promise you, I will disappoint."

His mouth twitched. "I like that you make me laugh. I want that." He ran his hands over her waist and hips. "Passion is a 'nice to have.'" He nodded at the wrinkled impression they'd left in the blankets on the edge of her bed.

"Not a deal breaker?"

"It's not." He sounded surprised by his own admission. "Don't get me wrong, I definitely want it. My mouth is watering thinking about all the ways I want to make love with you." His mouth twisted with self-deprecation while his hand drifted down to fondle her bottom. "But if that was all we had, if I thought I couldn't trust you, then no. *That* would be the deal-breaker. Trust is hard for me. It's going to take time."

She could understand that, given what he'd just told her, but she drew a slow breath that felt as though it spread powdered glass all through her chest.

"Given the way we started this relationship, I have to question how much I can trust you, too."

He acknowledged that with a stiff nod and moved his hands to her hips.

"Where does that leave us, then? With me sleeping in the other room?"

"No." The word escaped her as a barb of loss caught at her heart. She flashed her thick lashes up at him. "We're not going to learn to trust each other if we put walls between us."

"Or oceans," he said pointedly and started to draw her closer.

"No," she said, pressing away. "We have such different ideas of what a marriage means. I don't want to think about it anymore. I am washing off my makeup before you distract me again."

"Fine. I'll go brush my teeth. But Oriel." He caught her wrist. "If you want to sleep, tell me to stay in the other room."

She gave him her smokiest smile. "We'll sleep. Eventually."

Oriel had a rough start to her morning. They had slept, but not much. They might still be tentative about trusting one another, but between the sheets, she felt completely safe with Vijay. When she was with him like that, she felt, well, *loved*. It was kind of addictive.

When she woke and rose, however, she was tired and a bit achy and had to face the reality that sex hadn't solved anything. She was still pregnant by a man who was a bit of a mystery. Her life had still been cracked wide open by her birth family.

She barely swallowed her breakfast and was worried about it staying down by the time Vijay was placing the call to India.

"Do you want me to put it off?" he asked, frowning with concern.

"I think it's nerves." She had never felt so many caterpillars spinning cocoons in her middle.

His sister Kiran answered with a cheerful hello that immediately put Oriel at ease.

Thankfully, she had the excuse of a late night at her parents' party to explain any colorlessness on her part. It was also such an emotional call for both her and Jalil, bringing sharp tears to her eyes when she heard the break in his voice, that they could both hardly speak.

They kept it short, and she promised to be in touch soon to let him know when she might book a trip to meet him in person.

Afterward, she had a reactive cry in Vijay's arms, then pulled herself together and asked him to drive her to her childhood physician, where she was pronounced healthy and definitely pregnant. If her morning sickness became debilitating, she was advised to seek further medical attention. Otherwise, she should take her prescribed vitamins and consider scaling back her workload.

Oriel already knew she would have to do that, and it was eating at her.

"I know I don't *have* to work, but I've put in so much effort to get this far. Now my entire life is a row of dominoes that are falling over, one after another," she complained as Vijay drove her home. "I'll have to tell Payton to break my contracts. He'll want to tell the clients why, because some will say it's okay if I'm pregnant. Sometimes that works for their show or campaign. But I can't leak my pregnancy to the whole industry without telling my mother first. If I tell her, she'll want to know who the father is." She rolled her head on the headrest. "And what our plans are. Then there's your sister. I don't expect you to keep this from her, but will she tell Jalil? How will *he* react?"

"There is one more domino to consider."

"*No*," she said petulantly and turned her face away. "I don't want to hear it."

He pulled the car off the road to a spot that gave them a view of the river. The fronds of a willow dangled to play with the lily pads at the edge of the water.

"At some point your connection to Lakshmi will become public. You can put that off, but I doubt you can keep it hidden indefinitely, especially once you're in India. Her face is very well known. I recommend staying in front of the story to control how it rolls out. Once it's known, much will be made of the fact that Lakshmi was an unwed mother. Do you want to be judged for being the same?"

"That shouldn't matter! Not in this day and age."

"I agree." He held up a hand. "And to many it won't. To some it will be an affront. Unfortunately, those are the voices the media will amplify because that's what gains them clicks and revenue. I wouldn't want our child to suffer because we wished to make a point about free will."

"Ugh. What kind of a world are we bringing this baby into?" she muttered, bracing her elbow on the door and covering her eyes with her hand.

"Come. Let's walk a minute. Clear our heads. Is this the park your cousin teased you about last night?"

"Yes." She couldn't help a small laugh. She had forgotten about their childhood game in the pavilion of pretending to be a princess locked in a tower, taking turns rescuing the other.

"Show me." Vijay left the car and came around to open her door.

"I will not re-enact it," she warned, but enjoyed the short walk along the river's edge to the structure that overlooked the river. A family of tourists left it as they arrived.

"I don't know what I thought a knight in shining armor was supposed to save me from. My life was very simple and happy back then." She moved to the spot with the best view and curled her arm around the post. "Honestly, my life is not that difficult right now, just very unclear. I wish I knew what to do first."

"Oriel."

She looked over her shoulder.

Vijay was on one knee. He opened a ring box and offered it. "Will you marry me?"

She slapped her hand over her mouth, but a muffled squeak of shock came out. Inexplicably, tears came into her eyes. She wouldn't have expected to be so moved by a proposal from a man she had really only known a few days, but she was.

"How did you...?" She came closer. The ring was lovely. Modest, but eye-catching with its center diamond surrounded by smaller ones in a daisy pattern, all set in yellow gold. It looked like an antique. "Is that a family ring?"

"I went shopping while you were with the doctor. The jeweler said it came to him through an estate sale. It was likely made in the middle eighteen hundreds, but its provenance is mostly unknown."

As she had been for much of her life.

Her throat closed and her eyes grew hot. She could hardly speak.

"You're a romantic," she chided.

"I am not," he said with indignation. Then, with gentle affection, he added, "But I think you are, given your games here. I don't know what sort of white horse or dream castle I can offer you that you can't buy or make or achieve for yourself, but we're going to be a family. I think we can make a strong one if we go all in. I think we can make it work, even though it won't be ideal."

That was really what a family was—wholehearted, unconditional commitment. She knew that. It was how she already felt toward their child, and she believed he felt the same. It only made sense that they would close that final link between them.

The hollow pang that had sat in her heart all her life said, *But he doesn't love you, and he's said he won't be able to love you too.* It hurt quite a lot to acknowledge that, especially when that same ache made her fear she would never be loved, that there was some flaw in her that made it impossible for her to be cherished the way she longed to be.

That was something she had to resolve within herself, though. She had to believe she was worth being loved and not put it on others to prove it. Besides, maybe Lakshmi hadn't been given a choice about giving her up. By revealing that, Vijay had already gone a long way to helping her heal all those old insecurities inside her. She was grateful to him for that.

The even starker truth was, even if he never loved her, she knew she could love him. She was already halfway there. Maybe he hadn't been completely honest when they first met, but in the time since, he'd been considerate and protective and open in a way that must have been difficult for him. She admired the man he'd made of himself and knew she wasn't done learning who that man was.

It was terrifying to let her heart make such a huge decision for her, but she moved to perch on his bent leg and cupped his stubbled jaw. Her voice shook with unsteady emotion.

"Yes, I will marry you, Vijay."

He closed his arms tightly around her. His hot mouth captured hers. It was sweet and so intense it would have been frightening if he hadn't been so tender about it.

As tears of joy and trepidation burned behind her closed eyelids, she heard a faint cheer go up.

They broke away to see the family of tourists had been watching from a distance.

She and Vijay tipped their heads together in embarrassed laughter. Then he grasped her close to balance her while he got them both upright on their feet.

As he slipped the ring onto her finger, he said, "I'd prefer to marry as soon as possible."

"I have a few days of vacation left." She wrinkled her nose. "How do you feel about eloping?"

"Done."

CHAPTER EIGHT

THEY MARRIED IN a brief civil ceremony in Gibraltar. Oriel wore a cream-colored skirt with a pale rose top that set off the golden tones in her skin. Vijay was in a gray suit and tie. Their wedding was short, solemn and profound. Vijay hadn't approached his marriage lightly, but he hadn't expected such a depth of pride and satisfaction once their rings were on their fingers, either.

It felt like a beginning, a fresh one that held more promise than he'd allowed himself to believe in for a long time.

They returned to the chateau, where they called Kiran. She happened to be with Jalil, so they told them their news at the same time they told Oriel's parents. Everyone was ecstatic to hear a baby was on the way.

"I'm going to be an auntie." Kiran clapped with delight. "I can't wait to hug my very own sister!"

"I'm excited for that, too, but I have commitments in New York," Oriel said with an apologetic glance at Vijay. She had told him that as they'd been on their way to the registry office. "I have to meet with my agent, tell him everything that's happened. Figure out what my career will look like moving forward."

"Oh, but… Vijay, I thought you were coming home?" Kiran asked.

"I am." He had barely finagled this week in France as it was. The building up of the Asian division was fully underway, and he'd been paid to ensure it went smoothly.

He didn't like starting their marriage apart, though. It felt like they were getting off on the wrong foot, and his worst niggling doubts had resurfaced. He was trying to tell himself this was the sort of test that would be good for them in the long run—provided they passed it—but the separation still annoyed him.

"Vijay is bringing copies of everything my parents have on my adoption," Oriel said. "Perhaps you and Jalil can find something that ties back to Gouresh Bakshi. My parents are happy to make inquiries on this end, but we don't want to misstep and tip him off that you're investigating how he might have behaved with Lakshmi."

Jalil was pleased with that lead, and they soon signed off.

The rest of the day was relaxed, and Vijay tried not to think about the fact that they were flying in different directions the next morning, but when they made love that night, they were both more aggressive than usual. Oriel laid claim to him with her mouth and hands. He did everything he could to imprint on her that they were one.

They were both sweaty and near comatose after, but she woke him in the night, kissing him with a frantic urgency that lit his fire all over again.

He pried her nails out of his hair and pressed her hand to the mattress, pinning her with his weight. "What's wrong?"

"I'm afraid something will happen and I won't see you again."

"This won't be like last time." He sucked flagrantly on her earlobe and settled himself with proprietary ease between her soft thighs. "You're my wife."

He was an absolute Neanderthal because he loved saying that. *My wife. Mine.* "I would travel the world to come after you now. Don't you know that?"

"I've always been fine traveling on my own. I *like* not answering to anyone, but it suddenly seems very lonely."

"You're not alone, *priyatama.*" He shifted so he could roam his hand across her stomach. He circled her navel with his thumb, then caressed up to her breast, cupping the warm swell. They kissed long and slow.

When she reached between them and guided him, he pressed into her heat.

They stayed locked like that a long time, shifting here and there, mostly kissing and caressing and reinforcing their bond. When he heard the sweet moan reverberate in her throat and her sheath clenched hungrily around his erection, he gave them both what they were aching for. He began to thrust with tender power.

As the storm brewed, he felt her growing tense beneath him.

"Wait," he commanded raggedly, wanting them to hit the peak together. His lower back tingled, and a feral noise gathered in his throat. *"Now."*

Her voice broke on a scream of agonized pleasure. They seemed caught in the stasis of orgasm for eternity. Wave after wave rolled through him while her body milked at his. He lost track of which one of them convulsed or moaned, which sobbed or made wordless noises of bliss. He knew only that they were in this singular place together.

And when they parted the next day, he went home with an empty ache inside him far bigger than the one she'd left in him last time.

A morose cloud descended on Oriel the minute she left Vijay. By the time she was in New York, she was struggling harder than she ever had in her life to find a smile.

Her priorities had completely shifted. Her mind was around the other side of the planet, wondering what her husband was doing. Her most important goal had become a need to put down roots so her baby would have a home when they arrived. All of her work commitments became obstacles to what she really wanted.

She sat down with Payton two days after arriving and told him everything.

His jaw went slack, but he was very understanding.

"I wouldn't be doing my job if I didn't point out that you could capitalize on the connection," he said in the middle of their discussion.

"No," Oriel said firmly. "I know how many doors a famous mother opens, but I don't want to do that to Lakshmi. I have a feeling she's been exploited enough. No, the baby will be my priority for the next year, at least. I want to scale back. Cancel everything you can. If that means I have to start from scratch when I'm ready to work again, so be it."

"You will never have to worry about that, but I hear what you're saying." He promised to begin making calls.

She phoned Vijay from the car afterward.

"You sound upset," he noted. "I thought you were going to try to work while you were pregnant, not choose the nuclear option."

"Yes, but as I sat there, I knew this was what I wanted. I'm teary because it was a big step, but it feels right. This way I can come to India and properly settle in. I haven't stayed in one place for years."

"You can get to know this part of yourself before India knows who you are," he teased.

"Exactly. Has Jalil made any progress?"

"My sister, the frighteningly brilliant strategist, suggested Jalil send out letters to people who worked on Lakshmi's films, claiming he wants to make a biopic and request interviews. It's been a slow process tracking them down. A lot have retired or moved on to other things, but as word gets out in that community, Jalil expects more people will come forward."

"That's actually a great idea even if he didn't have an ulterior motive. I would love to watch something like that. Could her estate fund it?"

"I'll call him tomorrow and mention it."

"Okay— Oh. I'm having lunch with an old friend, and I've just arrived at the restaurant." The car pulled up to the curb. "He wants me to—"

"Tell me you're making my dreams come true." The silver-haired man who had been formulating exclusive skin care products for four decades opened her door.

"I'll text you later," she hurried to say to Vijay and ended her call.

She let Yosef help her from the car and kiss both her cheeks. He had hired her for her first magazine ad five years ago, and she wanted to tell him herself. "I'm sorry, but I'm going to break your heart. I'm going on hiatus from modeling. If you want me to pay for lunch, I completely understand."

Six days later, Oriel was exhausted. She had one more shoot tomorrow before she could finalize things with Payton and leave New York. She was in the middle of modeling skiwear, trying not to sweat makeup onto the furred hood, when one of the hovering assistants said, "There's an urgent call for Ms. Cuvier."

Her mind immediately went to her parents. Oriel unwound from awkwardly grasping a pair of skis while standing in fake snow and took the phone.

"Bonjour?"

"It's me," Vijay said in a hard, flat tone. "Payton is on his way with someone from TecSec. Don't leave until they get there. The news is out that Lakshmi was pregnant when she left for Europe."

"What? *How?*"

"A cameraman from one of Bakshi's film crews received Jalil's letter about a biopic. He decided to cash in and sold the story that she was pregnant in *My Heart Sings for You*. It was her last film before she went to Europe, and it came out when she got back. He said she was sick on set, and everyone suspected. He assumed Bakshi was the father."

They had already debunked that. Oriel's DNA test had said she had forty percent Scandinavian heritage. "Has Gouresh made a statement?"

"No one can find him, but Kiran has set up a bunch of alerts, and your photo is already turning up in subthreads remarking on the resemblance."

"No." She looked for somewhere to sit and sank onto a closed trunk that held equipment. "How is Jalil?"

"Worried about them finding you before we have a chance to put protections around you. So am I. Payton said he can get you out of your last shoot if you want to. I'd like you here where I can see to your fences and firewalls myself. The alternative is the chateau, but…"

"Maman is starting a new tour. I'd rather be with you."

"Good. I'll start making your travel arrangements. Watch for a text."

She ended the call and handed the phone to the assistant.

"Is everything all right?"

"Not really," she said in a daze. "Let's get what we can before I have to leave."

Vijay's new partner and the founder of TecSec, Roman Killian, arrived with Payton. Payton finalized the cancellation of her last contracts, and Killian escorted Oriel to her mother's apartment, where she hurriedly packed. Then he brought her to the TecSec jet. His wife, Melodie, and their two children were already aboard.

Melodie was excellent company, and the toddlers provided a lovely distraction on the flight to Paris, where the family disembarked. Each of the children gave her a big hug that jump-started all of Oriel's maternal instincts.

From there, she traveled with only a security detail and slept most of the way to Mumbai. By the time she was asked to sit up because the plane was descending, she had almost forgotten why she'd left New York in such a scampering hurry. She hadn't found much online about Lakshmi's possible pregnancy except a few sensationalized posts on gossip sites.

Oriel had been reading up on her biological mother every spare moment, absorbing the details of Lakshmi's life with greedy fascination, and had watched a few films with subtitles. Everything reinforced that Lakshmi had been very popular and treasured as well as a talented singer and performer, but she seemed mostly a South Asian phenomenon, not known well internationally.

Watching her was a surreal experience. She seemed familiar, yet everything about her was completely different from the life Oriel had lived or the person she had believed herself to be.

Now Oriel was landing in a country that, under different circumstances, would have been her nation of birth. Her identity. She was eager to discover if it felt like home, but a greater uncertainty confronted her.

It was hitting her that she had completely overturned her life to be with a man who was still very much a stranger. As an only child, and one who had begun traveling for her career when she'd still been in school, she had a very independent spirit. It would be one thing to reshape her future around the love of her life. It was quite another to do it for passion. What if she'd made a horrible mistake?

Landing under low, soggy clouds that looked cold and unwelcoming did not reassure her. Where was the undo button for life? She had a sudden urge to backspace all the way to Milan and make different choices.

Not true, she assured the baby, patting where apprehensive butterflies were taking flight in her belly. She peeked out the window and saw Vijay on the tarmac below, stepping from an SUV with a practiced pop of a wide black umbrella.

The air hostess pressed a button to lower the hatch that formed the stairs, and a dozen impressions hit her at once.

The temperature wasn't cold, merely rain-fresh cool. A gust brought in the fragrance of washed tarmac and wet earth. The patter of the rain was steady and musical, the humidity so tangible, her deep inhale rehydrated her, filling her with buoyant excitement.

And here was Vijay, taking the stairs in an easy stride, arriving in the opening with the umbrella so he provided a shelter to step into. Masculine scents radiated off him with the warmth of his body—spice and coffee and the damp cotton of his shirt as she stepped out of the plane.

She paused there, drinking in everything about this moment so she could remember it forever. She memorized the lights in the puddles and the green in the distance and the way her husband looked down at her, face filled with intriguing angles.

He took her breath away when he looked at her in that hooded way, holding his sensual mouth so tense and serious. His dark lashes flickered as he stole a very swift, proprietary glance to her toes and back, revealing nothing about his thoughts.

Even so, as she stood close to him, spatters of rain pelting them with the changeable wind, she felt as though she had arrived home—not because this country was in her blood, but because he was.

She had missed him. This was the place she *had* to be. It was a profound realization and yet one more way she was losing a piece of herself to the unknown.

If he had kissed her then, she would have laughed with joy, but a gust caught the umbrella and tipped it, sending a cold drizzle down her bare arm, startling her.

"Monsoon," he said. "Welcome to India."

She was so wrapped up in wanting him to show some sort of affection, she briefly thought the word was an endearment. As she realized her mistake, she ducked her head and wiped the trickle from her arm, embarrassed that she was behaving like a pubescent child wishing for a paper valentine.

The truth was, she wanted a lot more. She was falling in love with him, she realized with a catch of alarm.

It was too soon, too spontaneous, too *new*. It made her terrifyingly vulnerable when she had already sacrificed everything, but her heart had opened itself to him of its own accord. She had quit her old life because she wanted to be here, with him.

And his reception to all of that seemed very lukewarm.

Why don't you want me? Why don't you love me?

She tried not to be crestfallen, but she was.

"You are a true Mumbaikar if you're willing to stand in the rain instead of running to where it's dry." He nodded an invitation for her to move ahead of him down the narrow steps.

She dredged up an uncertain smile to cover her disappointment. "I am ruining an expensive pair of shoes."

Rain hit her ankles beneath the cuffs of her snapping wide-legged pants as she descended. Her sleeveless, light-knit mock turtleneck left her arms bare to the spits and spats that whipped off the breeze and stung her skin.

"Jalil has arranged a press conference at a hotel near here," Vijay said as they settled in the SUV. "You're up for it?"

No. She wanted to go somewhere private to re-evaluate all her life choices, but she didn't think she had the option to refuse.

"Of course." She had already approved the press release and memorized the statement she would make. "I warned my parents what was happening, but do you really think people will care that much? I mean, beyond reporters."

He looked at her as if she was very naive. "I do. Yes."

He didn't say anything else, but it wasn't far to the hotel. Their car was met in the parking garage by four burly, expressionless men. *Four.* Plus two people wearing hotel security badges.

They were shown through a private corridor and past an open door to a kitchen, where a curious silence fell as they walked by. An excited babble rose in their wake.

She looked to Vijay and noted that his whole demeanor was on alert.

"Kiran wanted to be here, but I asked her to stay at the office so I can give my full attention to you and your safety."

She began to realize he was actually *working*, wearing the role of protector in the most basic way. It was sweet, but she grew intimidated as they approached what sounded like a thousand voices beyond a wall. She unconsciously tightened her hand on the crook of his elbow.

As they reached a pair of doors where a handful of people were waiting, one looked up and made a noise of surprise.

Jalil turned and did a double take. He covered his mouth, and his dark eyes filled with tears. *"Beti,"* he breathed as he held out his hand to her. "You look just like her."

"Please don't make me cry." She caught his hand in both of hers. "Not yet."

They both laughed emotively, and he squeezed her hand so hard her rings dug into her fingers, but the pain helped her keep hold of her composure.

Someone offered to touch up her makeup while Jalil went into the room. The babble of voices nearly knocked her over, but they abruptly went silent as he was introduced.

Jalil began to speak in Hindi.

"He's explaining that he had suspicions Lakshmi had a child," Vijay translated for her. "And that she gave up the baby to protect her career, that she feared she and her baby wouldn't be accepted if she kept it."

"I can only speak English or French," Oriel whispered in belated panic.

"English is fine. When Jalil called this, he said most of it would be conducted in English. Now he's saying he's confident Bakshi was not the father."

"Has Bakshi been found?"

"No, he's still in hiding." He cocked his head. "He says he has confirmed that Lakshmi had a daughter because he has found her. You're up."

Oriel's knees wanted to give out. She swallowed the worst stage fright of her life. *It's just a runway.*

Walking for an audience had never bothered her beyond a few twinges of nerves, but her entire body became encased in ice. Her limbs felt disjointed as she allowed Vijay to escort her into the ballroom.

A collective gasp rippled over the hundred or so assembled reporters. Cameras flashed in a violent strobe. A babble of incomprehensible questions assaulted her ears.

She wore a resemblance, she told herself, in the same way she often wore an haute couture gown. That was what people were looking at, not her.

Her training came to her rescue, and she managed an aloof confidence as she joined Jalil at the podium and flashed her warmest smile.

"Good afternoon," she said as Vijay's men stepped in front of the microphone.

The room fell silent again.

"If you were surprised to learn that Lakshmi Dalal gave birth to me, you know exactly how I feel."

It was exactly the right note of humor and humanity to win them over. The flashes continued, but she felt the shift in the room. The acceptance.

She read her statement and took a few questions. Then Jalil's people ended the conference by providing contact information for further questions. As she walked out, someone was asking the reporters to please respect their privacy.

Jalil came with them in their car so they could have a few more minutes to chat. He knew she had been traveling for nearly a full day and needed time to take all of this in, so they made a date to have dinner with him and Kiran in a few days' time.

As she and Vijay were dropped off, Jalil said he would continue on to "make a report to Kiran."

"Make a report," Vijay scoffed as they entered the elevator with the doorman who brought her luggage.

"Does it still bother you that they're involved?" she asked.

"No," he allowed. "Jalil is insisting they take their time because he worries about the age difference."

"So did you," she reminded him.

"True, but I've since seen that their personalities are well-suited. If they wished to marry, I would support their decision."

He was speaking very objectively, reminding her of the night he'd asked her what her expectations of marriage were. Passion wasn't a deal-breaker, he had said, but she had hoped it was still alive between them. So far, desire seemed the furthest thing from motivating his urgency in bringing her here.

Doubts were digging claws ever deeper into her as he opened the door into a penthouse and thanked the doorman, instructing him to leave the luggage in the entranceway.

"Oh. Wow."

Vijay had told her over their daily video chats that he had found an apartment they could live in right away, with the option to buy. From the outside, the building had looked unremarkable, but this was a tasteful, modern oasis with endless views of the sea.

"It was renovated last year by one of our clients. It was actually two units and he combined them." Vijay pointed at the loft to indicate it had two floors. "I made him an offer on condition you approve."

If she hadn't been feeling as though there was an invisible wall between them, she would have thrown her arms around him and squealed with delight.

The decor was understated, the furniture chic but comfortable. Sliding walls of glass were the only separation between indoors and the wide terrace that overlooked the Arabian sea. The dining, living and kitchen area were all one airy space with plenty of room for Kiran's wheelchair if she decided to come live with them.

Oriel and Vijay had discussed it, and Oriel had no problem with sharing their home with Vijay's sister. She had often roomed with complete strangers at different times and always made it work. Once the baby came, she would probably be very glad for an extra pair of hands. Besides, judging from the way things were going with Jalil, Kiran wouldn't be with them for long.

For now, Kiran had chosen to stay in the lower level of a duplex that she and Vijay had called home for several years. The neighbors all treated her like family, and the home itself was fitted for her chair. Plus, Kiran said she wanted to give the newlyweds their privacy.

For what? Oriel had to wonder uneasily.

There was an elevator to the upper floor, but they walked up the floating staircase to a loft with a small sitting area beneath a skylight. They passed two spare bedrooms and a home gym before entering a master suite fronted by a wall of glass. It opened onto a private terrace that had a small landscaped garden as well as another stunning view of the sea.

Oriel moved to the part of the rail that was protected by an overhang and instantly imagined walking out here every single morning, drinking coffee, tasting the day.

"You're not saying anything." He was still wearing that watchfulness. She was beginning to think it had less to do with his security persona and more to do with whatever was going on in his own head. But what was *that*?

"It's incredible," she said with a reluctant smile. "You know it is."

"The security system is first class," he said dryly as he joined her at the rail. "The location is excellent. One of the best maternity hospitals in the city is nearby."

"That's good," she murmured.

They both stood there watching the rain.

"Oriel—"

"Do you want me here?" she asked over him.

"What?" He angled to look down his nose at her. "Of course." His voice was brisk, though, and his gaze went out to the gray horizon, where low clouds hung against chopping waves. "Why do you ask?" His demeanor was as cool and colorless as the rain.

She felt callow admitting it. Defenseless because she couldn't hide the fact she was hurt. "You didn't…kiss me when I arrived."

Thankfully, he didn't laugh at her. She might have gone straight back to the airport if he had. Even so, as he looked at her with vague bewilderment, a scorched self-consciousness rose behind her breastbone.

"We're not like Europe. Public affection isn't customary here."

"Oh." She hadn't even thought of the cultural differences she would face with this move. She might look like she had been born here, but she was French. Being demonstrative in public was very natural to her. "I have a lot to learn."

"We're a nation of people who live in multigenerational homes, so it's kept behind closed doors out of respect for our elders. I honestly don't recall ever seeing my parents kiss, not because their marriage was arranged. It just wasn't done."

"Oh." She started to relax, but realized, "You still haven't, though." Fresh shyness struck, and her cheeks stung with a painful blush. "Kissed me, I mean."

"I know." His voice had returned to being clipped. He moved back to the door into the bedroom.

Her heart lurched at the way he was putting that distance between them.

He lightly tapped his loose fist on the frame. "I hate myself for asking, but I have to." He pinned her with his steady gaze. "Who was he?"

She was taken aback. "Who?"

"The man whose dreams you were making come true."

She shook her head. "I honestly don't know—"

"Lunch. You left Payton's office and you were going to meet an old friend for lunch."

"Yosef!" she recalled, then stood tall with instant outrage. "He's nearly seventy, Vijay. He gave me my first magazine shoot, and yes, I wore a negligee back then, but he never once made me feel cheap about it. Unlike *you*. Do you really think I was stepping out on you days after we married? *Mon Dieu*, when you said you didn't trust easily, you should have explained you meant there was none at all."

She tried to brush past him into the bedroom. He put out a hand to stop her, and she thrust his arm away. She glared at him, daring him to touch her again.

"I don't want to be like this," he said through his teeth.

"Then don't," she threw back at him and stalked toward the bed. "Should I feel the sheets?" She patted the blankets. "See if they're still warm from whoever *you've* been with?"

His mouth tightened. "I haven't been with anyone since you. There was no one between meeting you in Milan and finding you in Cannes, either," he clarified.

"Same." She flipped her hair over her shoulder. "Do you believe me?" Let him try and say he didn't.

"Damn it, Oriel, I had someone cheat on me. I know it's weak of me to be suspicious, but I can't stand the idea that I might not be seeing what's right under my nose." He rubbed his stubbled jaw before dropping his hands onto his hips. He stared out the open doors as though seeing a past he couldn't change.

She was still angry, but an even more insidious sense of threat crept into her.

"Who? How long were you together?"

"Her name is Wisa. We met at university and wanted to finish our degrees before we married."

"So you were…" She had assumed he would have a romantic history, but, "You were *engaged*?" She covered the sick knot that arrived in her middle.

"Yes. The wedding was days away when we called it off. She was sleeping with my best friend. I found out as the rest of my life fell apart over my father's crimes. The worst part is—"

That wasn't the worst part? She dragged her gaze up to his shuttered expression.

"I realized later that she had likely been steered toward me in an attempt to have influence over me when I took control of my father's business."

"Oh." She touched the night table for balance. "That is awful."

"I don't think she knew what was going on any more than I did." He brushed a tired hand through the air. "On the surface, we seemed very compatible, nothing to raise my suspicion. I was the heir to a successful company, and she was the daughter of a local politician. I took my degree in business with a minor in electronical engineering. She thought I should plan to go into politics. That was our only bone of contention."

Oriel was still reeling. He'd been days away from a wedding. Relationships didn't get that far unless hearts were involved.

Vijay shrugged out of his jacket and threw it onto a chair in the corner.

"After Kiran, Wisa was the first person I told about my father's business dealings. Initially she supported my going to the police, but as our friends began to distance themselves, and she realized her uncle might be implicated, I caught her on a call with Madin. It was obvious they were involved. She said it was my fault, that I had ruined our future. *Everyone's* future. That I *drove* her to Madin. We canceled the wedding, and she stuck me with the bills as a final slap in the face."

"Were you in love with her?" The question came out before she had fully braced herself for the answer.

He met her gaze unflinchingly. "I was."

Her heart plummeted like a shot bird. "Are you still?"

"No," he dismissed firmly. "But I'm suspicious of that emotion, as you saw with my reaction to Jalil's interest in Kiran." He pushed his hands into his pants pockets. "I can't help thinking it's a smoke screen that people use to get whatever it is they really want."

That's why he had asked her what she wanted from marriage. He didn't intend to give her his heart. It was a surprising blow. He didn't want to love her. Wouldn't.

She pressed a hand over the spot where she felt as though a knife was lodged in her chest. When she tried to speak, she had to gulp in air first.

"Love can be used like that," she acknowledged, hugging herself. "My first boyfriend was only using me to get close to my mother's theater connections." It still made her feel like the worst naive fool for not seeing it. "I fell for it because…" She worked to keep her mouth from turning down. "Because I wanted that *big* love. You know? *The one.*"

He flinched and looked away guiltily.

"Don't. This isn't about you and your limitations. This is something I want you to understand about me." She hunched up her shoulders defensively. "I've always struggled with not feeling that I was loved enough. Otherwise she would have kept me. Right?" Tears rose in her eyes.

"That's not true." His shoulders sank, and he came toward her, reaching to cup her elbows.

She pressed her hand to his chest, holding him off.

"Even if it was, you've seen how much my parents love me. They would do anything for me, which makes me feel even worse for having these fears. But it's a normal thing a lot of adopted children struggle with. We worry that we were at fault somehow. It's irrational and complex and confusing, but that's how I realized I was susceptible to letting that feeling take over. Ever since that boyfriend treated me that way, I've been cautious about giving up too much of myself. I don't like getting hurt, either."

He pulled his head back slightly as if her words had shaken him at some level. Then he gave a jerky nod of understanding. His hands tightened on her elbows.

"I was only asking a question. It wasn't an accusation. I don't think you're cheating on me. I just needed to hear from you that it was nothing."

"It was nothing."

"Thank you." His hands twitched as though he wanted to pull her close while still trying to give her space. "But Oriel, look at the lengths Jalil has gone to find you. He wouldn't have done that if his sister hadn't seemed tortured by losing you. You were wanted. You were loved."

Her composure crumpled, and she went into his arms.

He held her secure, stroking her and saying, "I

wanted to kiss you the second I saw you today. I want you all the damned time. Never doubt that."

She gave a small sob and looked up at him. "Even like this? All weepy and messy?"

He framed her face in his warm, broad hands. "All the damned time," he repeated.

"Then kiss me." She lifted on tiptoe and offered her tear-dampened lips.

He closed his arms around her and opened his mouth across hers. As his flavor seeped into her senses, all her reservations eased.

Then, as their kiss deepened, sharp need twisted inside her. Vijay slanted his mouth for a deeper seal, and between one breath and the next, their kiss yanked her into a maelstrom of want.

For one moment, he let her feel the ferocity of his desire as he plundered her mouth, arms tight as he crushed her hips into the aroused shape behind his fly.

He seemed to exert all his will as he made himself ease his hold and lift his head.

"You should get some rest. You must be tired."

"What happened to 'all the damned time'?"

With an agile twist, he had them both on the bed. "Oh!"

"Yes, oh." He tucked her beneath him. "If you are too tired, now would be a good time to say so."

"I'm a little bit tired. You might have to do all the work."

"That, my beautiful wife, would be my pleasure."

* * *

A few nights later, Vijay took Oriel to meet Kiran and Jalil at one of Mumbai's most exclusive restaurants. The pair had been over to visit twice already, and Vijay had been going to work, but Oriel had been staying in the penthouse while she acclimatized.

They'd also been making love nonstop because they couldn't seem to help themselves. He had no complaints about that, but he did suspect they were expressing themselves physically because they didn't know how to do it verbally.

He was still disturbed by what she'd said about wanting the "big" love. *The one.* He had known there was a romantic hidden deep inside her, but he hadn't appreciated how fragile her heart was. Her amazing front of confidence hid any hint of insecurities. He was glad she had spelled out for him where she struggled, but he was also—very hypocritically— frustrated that she had developed her own inner guards to protect herself. It made it that much harder for them to be sure of one another.

It would all come with time, he assured himself. For now, she was feeling cooped up, and he was eager to show her his city and show the world his wife.

Of course, she caused a stir the minute they hit the street.

It was more annoying than anything. They had a security detail. He wasn't concerned about her safety to any serious degree, but he suspected this would wear on her long-term.

At least the restaurant was used to catering to Bollywood celebrities and other high-profile clientele. It was candlelit with glinting reflections dancing off glossy floors and mirrored tiles in the wall mosaic. Partial walls of wooden slats absorbed sound and formed partitions that created pockets of privacy.

Heads turned as they were shown to their table, but Oriel seemed unfazed.

"You're taking this in stride," Vijay remarked as they settled at their table.

"The attention? I forgot it was for me," she said with a blink of bemusement. "The same thing happens when I go anywhere with Maman. I've learned to ignore it."

They all chuckled, and it turned into a pleasant, relaxing meal. They were finishing dessert when Kiran's smile stiffened.

"Someone must have posted that we were here. Why else would *she* show up?"

"Who?" Oriel asked.

Vijay knew without looking and stiffened, watching for Oriel's reaction as his past literally caught up to him.

"Vijay, Kiran." Wisa's voice was a smug purr. "What are you two doing in this part of the city?"

"Wisa. Madin." Vijay rose to greet his ex-fiancée and his ex-best friend, determined to be nothing but polite. "Please meet my wife, Oriel. And our good friend, Jalil Dalal."

"Ah, yes. Such a colorful story. It's everywhere." Wisa's gaze widened on Oriel as though she was an exotic animal, a curiosity, but something to be dismissed. "You do have a way of making headlines, don't you?" she said pithily to Vijay.

It was exactly the sort of sly, denigrating remark she and everyone else had made when he had refused to look the other way over his father's transgressions. Anything to put him down.

He was about to set her in her place once and for all when Oriel spoke up.

"Would you like a photo?" She sent a friendly nod to someone beyond Wisa.

They all glanced to see that an elderly woman in a saree was watching Oriel with a delighted smile of recognition.

"I'll come there." Oriel rose and brushed past Wisa, saying, "I don't want to offend her." She paused and set a delightfully possessive hand on Vijay's shoulder. "This would be a good time to make an escape, or I'll be here all night. You should buy their dinner, though." She nodded at Wisa and Madin. "Make it up to them that we can't stay."

"I'd love to."

The look on Wisa's face was worth whatever they charged to his credit card.

"That was savagely brilliant," he said when he and Oriel were in the back of his car on their way home.

"It's from my mother's bag of tricks. I felt petty resorting to it."

"You shouldn't. The family at the other table was happy." They'd been over the moon that their grandmother had been singled out and fussed over by a celebrity. "Wisa will think twice before driving across the city to make things awkward for us ever again."

"Holding on to a grudge like that suggests she still has feelings for you." She glanced across at him, eyes wary and watchful.

"Her uncle had to pay a fine and narrowly missed going to jail. I imagine she believes I still deserve punishment for that."

"Why? Her uncle was the one who broke the law," she muttered impatiently.

"Thank you." He reached across to squeeze her hand, so moved that his chest felt tight and he had to swallow a lump from his throat. "Anytime I have to revisit that episode in my life, I feel sick. I thought I was a law-abiding, principled sort of man and had to decide if I really was. It was sobering to be put to the test, and when I stood by what I thought was right, I was vilified and abandoned. It means everything to me that you didn't give her a chance to spit poison in your ear."

"I should have thanked her," she mused. "If she hadn't been so self-interested, you'd be married to her, and I wouldn't have you or our baby or know any of this about myself."

Neither would he, Vijay realized with a catch of

fierce possessiveness for her, their baby, and the life they were starting.

Recognizing that flashed a fresh light on all he'd been through, searing away much of his resentment and anguish. His ever-present shame died a final death, becoming cold, flaky ashes. From now on, it would be a bitter and sooty memory, but not one that still had the ability to scorch and burn him.

"But honestly?" Oriel said with annoyance. "She was kind of a bitch. 'What are you two doing in this part of the city?' Like she owns it. I don't actually feel bad for snubbing her."

He chuckled and tugged her across the seat, into his arms. "I felt great about it." In fact, he felt as though he was falling in love, and he wasn't that unsettled by the prospect.

CHAPTER NINE

As the days turned into weeks, Oriel had to concede that she and Vijay were very well-matched. Sexually, their compatibility continued to be an A-plus, ten out of ten. They could hardly keep their hands off each other.

They also complemented each other in broader ways. They began adding personal touches to their home by way of art and sculptures and were always in agreement. They hired a housekeeper and cook with minimal discussion and already knew what they wanted in a nanny.

She and Kiran got on as if they'd known each other all their lives, laughing and enjoying each other's company whether Vijay was in the room or not. He even brought her into the office to introduce her around. Everything was in disarray due to merging with TecSec, but she was fascinated and enjoyed seeing that side of his world.

In the hours when the rain let up, Vijay drove her to different parts of the city to help her get her bearings, and into the mountains, where everything was lush and green. They took a day trip to see the caves with rock carvings on Elephanta Island, and because it was mostly tourists there, they enjoyed one of their most relaxing, incognito days ever.

He worked a lot, which made her conscious of the fact she didn't, but he chided, "Your job is to build our baby. That's work."

So far being pregnant wasn't that hard. Her nausea had passed once she'd caught up on her sleep. Today they were having a scan, but it was purely routine.

"I have to go to Delhi for a few days," he said, reading his phone while they waited.

"When?" She instantly felt a pang of separation anxiety. It wasn't that she was emotionally dependent on him. She was genuinely falling in love with him and hated to be apart from him.

"Tomorrow."

"Can you tell me why? Or is it something confidential?" She was getting used to the fact that he sometimes couldn't talk about certain things.

"Dangerously boring reasons. There's a problem with wiring in the building we've leased and some HR issues that need massaging. I'd ask you to come, but I won't have time to show you around. You'd be stuck in a hotel room."

"And I would miss my language class." She was going three times a week and practiced diligently with Kiran and their housekeeper. The classes were more than a determination to explore her roots, though. It was a nice reason to get out of the house, something she did for herself that wasn't wrapped up in her husband, and she was making some pleasant friendships with the eclectic expats she was meeting.

The ultrasound technician arrived, greeting them cheerfully. As Oriel stood, the young woman made a noise of amused surprise, then consulted her notes.

"Eighteen weeks? Is that a typo?" She made a perplexed face at Oriel's still flat middle.

"I'm very tall," Oriel pointed out defensively.

She had already had a small lecture from one of Kiran's well-meaning friends about ensuring her calorie intake was high enough. No one seemed to realize how thin she'd been when she'd gotten pregnant. The amount of weight she'd gained was right on target, and she was actually thickening around the waist and showing fullness in her breasts and face.

Plus, "My waist is long. There's lots of room for a baby to hide in here."

For one second, Vijay's expression seemed arrested, but he shook it off so quickly, Oriel wasn't sure if that had really been a moment of suspicion coming into his head.

"We'll confirm your dates," the woman assured her.

I know when I conceived. Oriel bit back the words.

A short while later, her affront was forgotten as the blurry image of their baby appeared with its heart pitter-patting.

Her eyes filled with tears, and so did Vijay's. As

they touched their trembling smiles together, she was so happy at having this little miracle inside her, she almost told him she loved him. Because she did. And she didn't know which made her heart overflow more, their baby or him.

New Bride with an Old Flame?

Vijay stared at his screen, annoyed by the unsavory headline, but more bothered that his team was taking this seriously enough they'd forwarded it.

They had a team who filtered through all the false sightings, many of them easy enough to disprove when they claimed Oriel was in New York and she was clearly here, but this one was from the days shortly after Vijay had met her in Milan.

It was a photo of Oriel at a restaurant table with a man who had a healthy head of dark hair and the shoulders of a thirty-year-old.

The shot was actually a screengrab from a selfie video posted by someone visiting New York and dining at an upscale restaurant. As Oriel's notoriety had risen, this tourist had realized she had inadvertently caught a celebrity in the background of her vacation vlog. Now the woman was claiming her ten minutes of adjacent fame by circulating the shot on the gossip sites.

In it, Oriel was leaning in, smiling playfully while delivering a flirty look through her long, thick lashes. It was unmistakably her. Vijay knew that curve of her cheek, the ripple in her hair that caught the light. He knew that adoring expression and had started to believe she only ever showed it to him.

He checked the date stamp and was further irritated to see it had been taken in the days after they'd been together in Milan. He told himself he had no right to the soul-eating jealousy that was trying to consume him, but he had a right to the truth. She had told him she hadn't been with anyone except him since Milan. And that the "old friend" she had lunched with had been a man in his seventies.

There was also that niggling moment at the ultrasound the other day, when the technician had remarked on Oriel not looking pregnant *enough*.

Back in Cannes, Oriel had been offended when Vijay had suggested the baby might not be his. *Of course it would be yours. Don't be rude!*

But she had gone back to New York after Milan. Had she seen—he read the caption—Reve Weston, New York billionaire, while she was there?

"Sir—"

"I need a few minutes." He abruptly closed the door of the empty office he stood in, cutting off the babble of voices down the hall.

He wanted to jump on a plane back to Mumbai, but things were still in disarray here in Delhi. He couldn't wait and wonder, though. He called Oriel for a video chat.

"Hi!" She was in her yoga clothes, hair bundled messily atop her head. "How's it going there?"

"Terrible. I'm sending you a photo."

"Of?"

"You. Having lunch with a man. In New York."

She frowned. The screen briefly went black. "What? *Mon Dieu*, that's not me." She came back onscreen. "Or it's been altered to make it look like it's me." She was frowning with concern, but not guilt, as far as he could tell.

"You don't know him?"

"I know who Reve Weston is. Every straight woman or gay man in New York does. He's one of those wealthy tycoons everyone dreams of catching. Is that what I'm up against now?" Her mouth twisted with annoyance. "People putting my image into photos to manufacture clickbait?"

"I ran it through Kiran's program, Oriel. It hasn't been edited. It was taken a few days after we met in Milan."

"Vijay." There was enough shock and hurt in her tone to cause him a trickle of compunction. "I thought we were past this."

"I'm not angry." He was trying not to be. He was trying to give her the benefit of the doubt. "I just want you to be honest about it. Tell me if you had a relationship with him and saw him again when you went back. Either time."

"Either...? Are you asking if I went on a date with an old boyfriend after you and I were married? No, I did not. I have never had lunch with Reve Weston. Ever. Or dinner. Or breakfast the morning after a night before. Please tell me you are not accusing me of getting pregnant by another man and passing it off as yours!"

"I'm just trying to get to the bottom of this."

"We are definitely hitting rock bottom if we're here," she snapped. "I'm sitting here eating my heart out, missing you because I love you so much, and you call to accuse me of *that*?"

His heart lurched. *I love you.* They were words he had told himself he didn't want or need to hear. His scorned self from years past warned him she might only be saying it to throw him off her affair, but his gut told him that was wrong. She meant it.

"You're punishing me for Wisa's infidelity," she accused, expression contorted with hurt.

The last thing he ever wanted was to hurt her, but he said, "I'm simply asking for an explanation for what is right in front of my eyes."

"I can't explain it," she cried with frustration. "But the fact you jump to the worst possible explanation tells me what you think of me, doesn't it?" She ended the call.

It was as though she'd stabbed clean through the screen and jabbed a hole in his chest. Vijay swore and pocketed his phone.

Oriel hadn't spent much time looking herself up online. She knew that way lay madness, and Vijay had people screening all of that, but in her hurt and fury, she began going down rabbit holes on Lakshmi fan forums. She found threads by dozens of people claiming to also be the product of Lakshmi's illicit liaison and therefore entitled to her fortune. Some of the posts were clear fakes, others credible look-alikes.

Some of it was very unsavory, but so was being accused of infidelity by her husband. She kept searching and came across another photo that claimed to be of her, this one more recent. It showed three frames in which she supposedly had an altercation with a photographer that ended with the man clutching his bleeding nose.

Cuvier Clocks Cub Reporter for Catching Her Canoodling

"With who?" she cried.

The woman in the photo was a really good double. She had a streak of pink in her hair, but her face and body were uncannily similar. The shocked, fear-filled look on her face was what really got to Oriel. She felt that other woman's emotions as if she was staring at her own reflection in a mirror.

Disturbed, she went back to the photo of the woman with Reve Weston and started searching for more of the couple together. She didn't have much luck until she stumbled across a list of guests from a gala that said Reve's plus-one had been someone called Nina Menendez.

When Oriel searched Nina's name, she discovered the woman's social profiles had been locked down. The only thing she was able to turn up was—weirdly—from a fashion degree program at a college in New Mexico. Nina appeared in a video from four years ago.

Oriel's skin broke out in goose bumps as she listened to Nina speak. She sounded just like her!

"I go for my first job interview on my twenty-first birthday next Thursday. No matter how that goes, I plan to have my first legal drink after. Wish me luck."

Oriel glanced at the date, and her heart nearly came out of her mouth. Nina's birthday was the day after Oriel's, but Oriel had been born a few minutes before midnight. She knew because she'd been going through all the paperwork on her adoption with Jalil.

She and Nina were essentially the same age.

"Mon Dieu, mon Dieu..." she heard herself muttering, her skin going hot and cold as she hurriedly read the rest of Nina's bio on the college website.

She was barely able to make sense of it. Nina mentioned her father's military career as inspiration for some of her designs, adding that her father had been stationed at one of the bases in Germany when she had been born.

Oriel shakily opened another tab on her browser and punched in the distance between the air force base and the small village in Luxembourg where she'd been born.

One hour and seven minutes by car.

Impossible.

For a long time, she sat without any coherent thought in her head. The words *I should call Vijay* drifted into her head, but faded before she could act on them. She had the sense that Kiran could do some intensive digging, but Kiran would feel compelled to tell Jalil. Oriel didn't want to cause the older man any further upheavals if she was being delusional.

Was she? The truth seemed as plain as the identical nose on Nina's face. She didn't know if she wanted to laugh or cry or check herself into a hospital for possible hallucinations.

When Oriel realized it was the middle of the afternoon in France, she called Max, barely stammering out, "Do you have access to any sort of database that would give you background information on a designer in New York?"

"It's called gossip, *chou*. Give me a name and I'll have all the dirt within the hour."

She told him, and he called back forty-eight minutes later.

"Well, that was interesting," Max said cheerfully. "Mademoiselle Nina is an upstart who began working for Kelly Bex a year ago. The party line is that she showed promise, but was ultimately a disappointment. The truth is, she stole a hunky billionaire, Monsieur Reve Weston, from the maven Bex herself. *That's* why she was fired, thrown onto the street, told never to darken their doorway again."

"Not so much a lack of talent, then."

"*Oui*. Because she does have talent. This was much harder to pry from one of my nearest and dearest, but he claims to have seen some of her work. He expects it to be, and I quote, 'priceless when the designer is revealed.' I've looked her up. She looks just like you. Beware, *chou*. She may try to trade on that."

"She's still in New York?"

"No. Apparently, she flew to Paris on Weston's supersonic jet yesterday. He has a pied-à-terre—which is a monstrous two-story penthouse—on Avenue Montaigne."

"Merci, Maximus. Tu es mon héros." She hung up and, with her heart racing out of her chest, called her mother's assistant. If anyone could charter a flight to Paris within the hour, she could.

Every time Vijay reached for his phone, he became infuriated by their fight, by his vacillating trust, by the seesaw of wanting to believe her and not wanting to be a fool.

He set aside his phone and closed his eyes, but all he saw was Oriel looking at that other man with the love she had claimed to have for *him*.

Jealousy was such a lowering emotion. So insecure.

That photograph wouldn't bother him so much—that was a lie, but he told himself it wouldn't bother him this badly—if Oriel had owned up to the affair and assured him the relationship was over. Instead, she had denied the association even though she had been in New York after Milan and again after they'd married.

He wanted to ask Kiran to search the online archives for more photos of this bastard billionaire, to see if Oriel had been photographed elsewhere with him, but he was too ashamed. Ashamed of his suspicions, ashamed of what might turn out to be true.

Ashamed that he might have allowed himself to be taken in. Again.

He was trying to believe Oriel's word—another lie, but not entirely. He wanted to believe her. He did. But there was a piece of himself that couldn't let go of the past. He had failed to see reality when it had been deliberately obscured from him, so he had learned to keep his eyes open. There was *photographic evidence* to refute what she claimed.

What else could he think but that she had feelings for someone else? Feelings she wouldn't admit to?

The mere idea of it scraped out his chest far worse than Wisa's betrayal. He didn't want to believe Oriel would do that to him. They were far too close, closer than any relationship he'd ever had.

He *loved* her. He wouldn't be this tortured if he didn't. He loved her and he was anguished at the thought of her with a stranger, but he was being a fool. She was here in India, making a life with him, wearing his ring and having his baby.

What did he care what she had done in the past if she was here with him now? If she wanted another man, she would be with that other man. He shouldn't push her away with his rotten suspicions. Instead, he should be looking for another explanation.

He glanced at the clock, unwilling to wake Kiran to help him, but in the morning he would ask her to come to Delhi and take over for him. He would go home, make up with his wife, and figure out what the hell was going on.

His phone pinged, and he picked it up to see a text from Oriel.

Her name is Nina Menendez. She's in Paris. I'm going to see her.

CHAPTER TEN

ORIEL HAD SLEPT a little on the flight. Mostly her mind had been cracked in half by a thought that was even more outlandish than her being the secret daughter of a Bollywood star—that she might be the twin of one.

Vijay had texted her back, asking her to wait for him, saying he would go with her.

I'm in the air. I have my guards. I'm not leaving you, but I have to meet her. She might be my twin. Please trust me to come back. I love you.

There was no response to that, but she really hoped he would trust her. She was devastated by his accusations and didn't know how they would move forward if she was forever trying to prove herself to him.

Was she running away from him as impetuously as she had married him? A little. She'd been trying so hard to become a part of his world, which was her own world too, she supposed. But she had constructed a life with him because everything she had known about herself had been shattered. Now she might have yet another layer to unpeel, and she didn't know how to deal with it.

She entered her old flat with a desperate need for a sense of homecoming, the way it had always felt when she had returned from breaks between modeling gigs. Her parents had helped her buy this place when she had begun traveling for modeling, and she had been making the payments since. She had rarely spent more than a few weeks at a time here, but it was hers, and it was where she had always been able to relax and feel like herself.

It was also in a nice, secure building in the same arrondissement as Reve Weston's. She was only a short distance from him, she realized. A half-dozen blocks from Nina.

Oriel was so worked up, she only spent five minutes in her flat, just long enough to freshen up before she had her security detail drive her to Avenue Montaigne.

The paparazzi had posted photos of the building where "Oriel" was supposedly staying with Reve, so her driver found it very easily. She had one of her men escort her past the photographers, who snapped to attention as she left her car.

In the lobby, the doorman greeted her in English. "Mademoiselle Menendez. I understood you were away with Monsieur Weston."

For a moment, her heart pounded so hard she thought she might faint. Blood rushed in her ears and she recalled that she hadn't eaten since before she had landed.

I want Vijay, she thought.

"Elle n'est pas là?" She didn't realize she was speaking in French until the man grew alert with confusion at her native accent. "I'm Oriel Cuvier. When will they be back?"

He blinked with astonishment. "I'm sorry, but I couldn't say. Would you like to leave a message?"

She left all her contact details, and the paparazzi followed her home. She ignored them. She crawled into bed and noted that Kiran had texted.

I spoke with Vijay. I'm here if you want to talk.

Oriel thanked her and said she needed time to think. Then she called her mother, who was going on stage in Vienna shortly. Estelle was flabbergasted to hear there might have been two babies.

"I don't know why anyone would do something so hurtful as to separate a pair of twins. Our application would have said we wanted a single baby, but if they had told us you had a sister, we would have taken you both."

"I knew you would say that, but I needed to hear it."

"Can Vijay not help you learn the truth? He seems resourceful. He found *you*."

"We had a fight." She didn't get into the painful details of his accusations.

"A disagreement or a fight?" Her mother's tone grew serious.

"We're having trouble trusting one another. I'm worried we rushed into things."

"Of course you did, *chou*. It's always been your way to move quickly. You walk away just as quickly if something isn't right. Is that what happened? You've discovered he's not right for you?"

"Marriage isn't piano lessons," she said grumpily.

"This is true. But you know yourself, and if you have realized these piano lessons do not make you happy, then leave him. I'll support you."

Oriel laughed, but it was more an anguished sob, because her stomach clenched hard with rejection of that suggestion.

"No," she murmured. "He's the father of my child." He was *the one*. For her, at least. She didn't know how he felt. "We'll have to make it work." She only wished that she knew *how*.

"And that is also your way," her mother chided gently. "When you do find what feels right, you *commit*."

Oriel's heart swerved. Her mother was right. She had locked herself into a life with Vijay that would be nearly impossible to unravel. She didn't want to! But he didn't love her. Didn't trust her. She didn't know how to fix that.

"I'm about to go on, *chou*. Would you like me to sing for you?"

"It's been a long time since we've done that. Yes, please, Maman. I love you. Break a leg."

Estelle hadn't done this since Oriel was very young and missing her when she was away on tour, but she had her assistant keep the line open and prop the phone in a suitable place so Oriel could hear her while she performed.

Oriel fell asleep with her phone on the pillow and tears on her cheeks.

She awoke with a melancholy knowledge that Paris was no longer her home. She belonged in that other place, the one with a spicy fragrance in the air and sheets of rain falling from the sky. The place where a man stretched naked beside her in the morning and played with her hair when they watched TV in the evening.

Could they have that again? She didn't know, but not if she was here and he was there.

She texted Vijay.

I'm going to stay and list the flat.

It seemed a neutral enough means to open communication, but he didn't respond. It was the middle of his workday, though. He had a lot to get done in Delhi.

She called a property agent, then had boxes delivered and began sorting through her personal things. One of her guards was helping her take down a box of keepsakes from the closet shelf when her door buzzer rang, indicating someone was waiting outside.

The paparazzi had been pestering her periodically, so she asked him to leave the box on the kitchen table while he ran down to tell them to shove off.

She absently filled the kettle as she acknowledged that all this culling of her possessions was a time-filler while she contemplated the bigger unknowns in her life. How would she mend her marriage? What would happen when she returned to India?

The knock on the door sent her heart leaping.

It was probably the guard returning, she cautioned herself, but she hurried across the room. Had Vijay come? She didn't actually want him to come after her. She wanted him to trust her to return to him so they would have a foundation to build on.

She flung open the door with anticipation anyway and confronted a mirror.

Her reflection wore a different outfit, something in denim. Oriel wasn't taking in superficial details when there was so much else that was exactly *her*. The wave in her dark hair, her arched eyebrows, the shape of her nose and the flecks of greenish gold in her eyes. The way her jaw hung slack and her mouth worked to find words.

Oriel's mouth was doing the same. No coherent thoughts were coming to her. Her throat had closed, her chest was tight, and her whole body began to tremble.

There was a rushing sound in her ears, so a man's voice in the distance barely made sense. "I thought I should bring her up since you went looking for her yesterday. She was going to be mobbed downstairs."

She and Nina stared at one another for twenty-five years and nineteen weeks and three days and however many hours and minutes and seconds had passed since they had exited the womb they had shared.

Oriel didn't know how she knew that to be fact, but it was. This was her sister.

They took a step at the same time, hugging themselves back together again.

A whistling kettle broke them apart.

A different man's voice said, "I'll get that. You two sit down."

He nudged them inside and closed the door, then snagged a box of tissues from a table and held it between them.

That's when Oriel realized fat tears were dripping off her cheeks. She took a few of the tissues and sniffled, beginning to mop up. She watched her sister—*her twin*—do the same. They were both gasping and shaking in the same way.

They both smiled through all of it as they moved to the couch and sat. Still neither spoke. Each time one of them tried, each time they looked at the other, they welled up again. Oriel knew exactly how Nina felt. Her heart was too big for her chest. Her emotions were so expansive, her shoulders ached. There was a lump in her throat too sharp to swallow.

After a few minutes, Reve came back with two cups and set them on the table. Oriel couldn't have said what was in them, but Nina looked at him with naked love that she blinked away when he raised his gaze.

Oriel felt that agony of unrequited love inside herself, too. Amid this upheaval, her heart throbbed with want for Vijay. He wouldn't be able to do anything, but she wanted him here anyway, sharing this monumental moment with her.

She wanted him to squeeze her shoulder the way Reve did Nina's as he asked, "Do we need introductions? I'm Reve. This is Nina. I presume you're Oriel unless there's a third one?"

"*Mon Dieu*, can you imagine?" Oriel laughed into her handful of damp tissues.

"There's not," Nina said. "There are only two of us." She looked around, and Reve came from the door, where she had dropped her bag. She smiled her thanks at him again with that same glimmer of adoring love. "Reve and I were in Luxembourg, trying to find some answers about... Well, everything. Me. I didn't actually know my parents weren't my birth parents until you were making headlines and people started calling me by your name. I thought you'd think I was a crackpot if I didn't have some proof that we could be... It's weird to say it. Twins," she said with a teary laugh. "We raced back here when Reve's doorman sent the message that you were here in Paris and had come looking for me."

"Did you find the clinic? What did you learn?"

"We found some records from the doctor who delivered us." She sent Reve a look that held a scold, but started digging into her bag. "And we met a woman who was a maid at the house where Lakshmi stayed. I showed her a photo of Lakshmi's manager. She said it was him, that they claimed to be married, but she said they fought all the time. They spoke in Hindi, but she could tell he wanted her to give up the baby. Lakshmi didn't want to. She said Lakshmi wrote letters whenever he went out and threw them in the fire when he came home. The maid pulled this out of the grate one day. She wanted to know what was going on, but she didn't know what to do once she'd read it. Then Lakshmi delivered and they were gone."

"And she kept it all this time?" Oriel carefully unfolded the paper. It had been folded in four and was scorched where the corners had come together. Only the middle of the page remained, but she'd written in English.

…know we promised we wouldn't write. I hope your boy is improving…

…never wish to separate you from him, but want you to know…

…could marry him, but he says the baby will be white…

…midwife assures me all is well, but I sense she's hiding…

…and when it's time insists I must give it up…

…know what else to do. I wish you were here to…

"To our father?" Oriel bit her lips to keep them from trembling. It meant so much to know there had been love between them, even if it had been an impossible one. "This is so sad. My heart is absolutely broken for her."

"Me, too." Fat tears sat in Nina's eyes, and her voice cracked. "I don't think she got to see us or hold us or even know there were two of us."

They searched each other's eyes, anguished for the mother they hadn't known and the memories they had missed making as a family.

"My parents would have taken both of us if they'd been told. They're actually really excited to meet you," Oriel said with a small, quavering smile.

"Oh, my gosh, when I tell you how I came to be with my family…" Nina sent the heel of her hand across her cheekbone and glanced at Reve, seemingly at a loss. "We're going to need something stronger than coffee."

"We have more paperwork that we want to give to Lakshmi's family, too," Reve said.

"It's okay," Oriel said, waving Nina off from reaching into her bag again. "That can wait a few minutes. I want to know everything about you. I already know you're a fashion designer."

"And you're a model. It's like we're twins."

They laughed in a way that was eerily similar and that might have made them dissolve into fresh tears, but an abrupt knock on the door had them both twisting to look at it.

Reve ambled over.

"Ah," he said as he saw who was behind it. "The husband."

CHAPTER ELEVEN

IT WASN'T VIJAY'S worst nightmare, precisely, but he really wasn't thrilled when a man—*the* man—opened the door of his wife's flat.

Reve Weston was handsome, rich. At home. Smug.

"Vijay!" Oriel leaped to her feet.

Reve stepped aside, and Vijay saw Oriel's double stand and smile in a tentative greeting.

The resemblance was eerie and an easy mistake in a photo. In person he knew immediately which one was his wife. There were small, obvious differences. Nina's teeth were not quite perfect, and was that a streak of pink in her hair? She was a tiny bit shorter, but she was every bit as beautiful as Oriel.

Even so, rather than inciting a spark of sexual attraction in him, he only felt endeared toward her for her close resemblance to someone he loved. He didn't feel a gut-deep hunger and overwhelming need to connect or a stark, protective urgency to touch and reclaim intimate space the way he did toward Oriel.

"This is a plot twist, isn't it?" He moved into the sitting area and greeted Oriel with a light kiss on her cheek.

When in France, he conveyed when her lashes flicked up at him.

He hovered close enough to inhale her scent and absorb the light brush of her body against his.

She dipped her chin and rolled her lips together, indicating their conflicts were not resolved, but she stayed in the arm he looped around her waist. Her gaze up at him was not hostile, merely vulnerable and deeply uncertain.

He had hurt her. The knowledge squeezed his guts in a cruel fist.

"Vijay, this is Reve Weston and Nina Menendez." He heard the catch in her voice. Her joy was so visceral, it cracked something open in him. "My twin."

"That's what the birth records would suggest, at least," Nina said with shaken laughter as she took his hand.

"And anyone with eyes," Reve drawled.

"Still." Nina glanced back at him. "I imagine Lakshmi's family has been inundated with people claiming to be her daughter. I'm happy to do a DNA test."

"It looks like it will be redundant, but I've already connected with the lab we use here," Vijay said. "They have someone who can take the samples and rush the results. I'll make that call shortly, but…" He looked at Oriel, and whatever was in his face made her pupils expand and her lips tremble. "I need to speak with my wife."

"You should speak to your family, Nina. Things are going to get very chaotic when the jackals at the door downstairs realize there are two of you." Reve sounded grim enough that Vijay was put on high alert to threats he couldn't see.

Nina bit her lip and nodded with agreement, maybe remorse, but she smiled as she reached for Oriel. "I didn't mean to impersonate you. I've been trying to stay under the radar, but they're relentless."

"Vijay, you should arrange protection for her," Oriel said, looking to him.

"Already in the works," he assured her.

Reve shot him a glare that warned him to stay in his lane.

Vijay didn't flinch, and only said, "Do you think I'm going to let anything happen to my wife's sister?" He reached for his phone. "I'll have one of my guys lead you out through the maintenance entrance that I used to come in. Tell your car to meet you on the south side."

While he and Reve exchanged information, Nina asked, "Will you come for dinner? Now that I've found you, I don't want to miss another minute."

"Me, either," Oriel said emotively, but she looked to Vijay as if she knew they had things to talk out, too. "I'll text you in a little bit?"

"Perfect." They hugged each other so tightly, it added another layer of ignominy to Vijay's guilt over suspecting she'd lied to him.

The pair left, and Oriel stayed at the closed door, chewing her bottom lip as she regarded him. The space between them was a cavern of vipers and land mines, and the valentines of love she had sent him, which he had crumpled and stepped on.

"I apologize," he said sincerely. "I should have trusted you. I knew you wouldn't hurt me like that. In here I knew it." He tapped his chest. "Up here…" He tapped his temple. "But I won't let that happen again. I love you, Oriel."

He saw her jerk and heard her breath hiss in, but her expression only grew more anguished. His heart lurched as he realized he might have done irreparable damage to something that was becoming increasingly precious to him.

He took a step toward her, and she put up a hand.

"I'll give you a pass because there's no way you could have known I had a twin, but the fact is, you *don't* trust me, Vijay. And I can't fix that." She shrugged with despair. "And I can't spend my life worried about how you'll interpret everything I do, especially when there are people out there who will use my image and cast doubts and—"

"Shh. Stop."

He came forward a few more steps, but she kept her hand up to hold him off.

"I promised to come back and I *will*. Look around. I'm packing!" She waved at the full boxes on the floor, and at the bare walls. "I'm selling this flat. I'm going to live with the father of my child. I hope we can repair this marriage of ours, but you didn't even trust me to come back. Instead you've chased me here, and what did you think when Reve opened the door? That he'd just left my bed?"

"I thought I should have been here," he said fervently. "Because I made a promise to you when we learned you were pregnant that I would be here for you through all of this. I meant *all* of it. Not just the baby, but this. Learning who you are. You told me once that you always wished for a sibling. The minute I realized that's who she was, I knew you would be so excited, but also rocked to the core. *I* have questions, Oriel. You must be…"

His heart hurt for her, for all the anger and confusion she must feel at having been torn from the woman who gave birth to her *and* the sibling she should have had in her life all this time.

"Somewhere in there, you're wondering if you should have known that Nina was out there, aren't you? You think you should have found her long ago, on instinct or something."

"I think she knew before I did, but she didn't reach out. She said it was because she thought I wouldn't believe her, but…"

"I know." He came close enough to gather her in. "You feel cheated. And also guilty for wishing you'd had that other life where you grew up with her and Lakshmi."

She nodded while tears tracked down her cheeks.

"See? I know you, Oriel. More importantly, I *love* you. It kills me that I hurt you so badly, you felt you had to come here and face this alone."

Her eyes were leaking more tears. "I'm used to doing things on my own. I've told myself it was the way I liked it, but from the moment I left Mumbai, I've been thinking that I want you here with me, even though you can't do anything."

"I can do this." He folded his arms around her and held her, just held her and rubbed her back as she trembled.

Slowly she wound her arms around his waist and leaned on him, sighing out a lifetime of pent-up grief. He closed his eyes in gratitude.

"I love you, Oriel. I should have said it the first time you did. I've been sick with myself that I didn't. I know my heart is safe with you. *I know that.* It wasn't you I didn't trust. It was love. It hurts to love. It bloody *hurts* to love someone this hard. But I forgot that it heals, too. It gives a reason to hope and to push on when the rest of life is too bleak to face."

Vijay's hand stroked her hair, and his stubbled jaw rested against her cheekbone. A bubble of hope was trying to crack open her breastbone.

"Can I also say," his voice rumbled next to her ear, "that even though I understand your sense of urgency to meet Nina, and that you were hurt and angry with me, if you had trusted me just a tiny little bit more, you might have held the plane and let me come with you?"

She sniffled back her tears and looked up at him, chagrined. "Guilty."

"You probably would have had more faith in me

if I'd told you I love you." He slid her hair behind
her ear. "I do. So much." He looked at her as though
he was beholding something magical. "I've had to
beat and claw my way into the life I have. It didn't
seem like being this happy should be this easy, but I
won't give you a reason to doubt my feelings again."

"Me, either."

He touched her chin, and their mouths flowed
together in the simple, inevitable way they had between them. Perfect and tender and now an expression of that wider, deeper, heart-expanding emotion.

He took great care as he tightened his arms and
swept his mouth across hers, but his love was so
tangible in that kiss, she shook under the force of it.

"Come," she invited him, taking his hand and
drawing him into her bedroom.

They settled on the bed fully clothed, sharing
soft, soothing kisses that held no urgency because
this was love in its purest form. It was touch and
acceptance of their human flaws and celebration of
their perfection. Of their divine connection.

They were a special combination, though. One
that couldn't help but create passion when they were
together. Soon it was snapping like flames around
them, burning away a fold of collar so kisses could
extend down a throat. Demanding layers be removed
so they could rub their bodies together in the exquisite friction of animal desire.

But even when he slid into her with a carnal groan
and her body responded with a sensual clench, their
coupling was imbued with the intense love that em-

anated from their pores. She petted his spine and he sucked on her earlobe, but sweet light shone behind her eyes. His voice was hoarse with joy as he moved, telling her raggedly, "I love you. We belong like this. Always. Together."

That was how they crested the final peak. Together. Shattering in unison. Destroyed, yet rebuilt with pieces of the other embedded within their souls.

EPILOGUE

"I LOVE THAT she thinks I'm you, but she's hungry, so…" Nina spoke ruefully as she handed Lakshmi, whom they all called "Lucky," to Oriel.

The six-month-old began to nuzzle and root at Oriel's cheek. Thankfully, Oriel's sister, the genius designer, had been immersing herself in their roots by studying the construction of traditional Indian clothing. She had sewn Oriel's celebratory saree and included nursing snaps in the blouse. Oriel adjusted her *pallu* and settled her squirming daughter to latch on.

"Also, I have somewhere to be."

"Oh?" Oriel was teasing her, and Nina knew it. Her sister was an open book at the best of times, but they had a wonderful ability to read each other very well.

"Don't ask me," Nina pleaded with exasperation and beckoned someone from across the marquee tent.

Oriel chuckled. "Don't worry. I don't know what Maman has planned, only that it will be spectacular."

For anyone else, the bringing together of all these people for Oriel and Vijay's wedding reception would have been enough, but Madam Estelle was determined to outdo herself and make it a memory that would be talked about for years. Nina's family were here, along with Jalil and Kiran and other treasured connections from around the globe, all dressed in a mix of Western and Indian garb.

The courses of French and Indian cuisine had been amazing, and the tribute to Lakshmi had been heart-wrenchingly sweet. The marquee was draped in silk and strings of flowers. Everywhere there were tropical plants, a wild abundance of color, and spices lending fragrance to the air. There had been speeches, a song from Estelle, and a toast from Oriel's father that would live in Oriel's heart forever.

It was already a night of pure enchantment.

"Did you need me?" Vijay asked, his warm hand descending on her shoulder.

"No, I—"

"Yes," Nina corrected her. "Sit." She nodded at the spot on the love seat that had been Vijay's for most of the evening. Nina had stolen it when he had moved to the bar with Reve.

"She's more and more like my sister every day," Vijay remarked to Oriel as he retook his seat and brushed a light greeting across their daughter's curled fist.

Nina laughed, then poked her tongue out at him before she disappeared.

"What's happening?" Vijay asked.

"I have no idea, but I suspect we'll need…"

He was already fishing into the diaper pack for the baby earmuffs. He slipped them onto Lucky's head as the lights began to swerve all over the tent, gathering everyone's attention.

A firm thump-thump sounded on a *tabla* drum. A flute and sitar strings drew people in colorful sarees from all sides of the tent.

As Madam Estelle began to sing in Hindi, the dancers settled into a precise formation on the dance floor, beginning a slow, undulating walk. They were Oriel's cousins and Nina with her sisters, and there was Kiran among them, spinning her chair and raising her arms in a graceful ballet, giving her shoulders a shimmy before clapping her hands to pick up the tempo.

Vijay's arm closed around Oriel's shoulders, and he drew her tight into his side. She felt his chest expanding with laughing emotion, but they both had tears in their eyes.

"I could not feel more loved," he told her sincerely.

"Me, either," she admitted, deeply touched that her mother would go to all this trouble to celebrate this side of her daughter's life.

The energy picked up, and the dancers moved into more of a hip-hop style until the music abruptly cut off with a group clap.

A dozen people in suits abruptly stood. They wore serious expressions as they popped their collars, then pretended to spit on their palms before they smoothed their hair back on both sides. The music resumed in plucked strings as they sidled onto the dance floor.

"Will there be a rain machine?" Vijay asked.

"Don't put it past her."

It was a dance-off between gowns and suits, full of push and pull, defiant head tosses and waved scarves, straight out of a Bollywood musical.

Dying with delight, Oriel fell into her husband. "This is too much, but I never want it to end."

"It won't," he promised her. "The credits will roll, but we'll continue to live happily ever after."

"Promise?"

"I do."

She believed him.

*****

Couldn't get enough of
Married for One Reason Only?

Make sure to watch out for the next installment in
The Secret Sisters duet—
Manhattan's Most Scandalous Reunion

In the meantime, why not also get lost
in these other stories by Dani Collins?

Confessions of an Italian Marriage
Innocent in the Sheikh's Palace
What the Greek's Wife Needs
Ways to Ruin a Royal Reputation
Her Impossible Baby Bombshell

Available now!

#3941 THE WEDDING NIGHT THEY NEVER HAD
by Jackie Ashenden

As king, Cassius requires a real queen by his side. Not Inara, his wife in name only. But when their unfulfilled desire finally gives her the courage to ask for a true marriage, can Inara be the queen he needs?

#3942 MANHATTAN'S MOST SCANDALOUS REUNION
The Secret Sisters
by Dani Collins

When the paparazzi mistake Nina for a supermodel, she takes refuge in her ex's New York penthouse. Big mistake. She's reminded of just how intensely seductive Reve can be. And how difficult it will be to walk away...again.

#3943 BEAUTY IN THE BILLIONAIRE'S BED
by Louise Fuller

Guarded billionaire Arlo Milburn never expected to find gorgeous stranger Frankie Fox in his bed! While they're stranded on his private island, their intense attraction brings them together... But can it break down his walls entirely?

#3944 THE ONLY KING TO CLAIM HER
The Kings of California
by Millie Adams

Innocent queen Annick knows there are those out there looking to destroy her. Turning to dark-hearted Maximus King is the answer, but she's shocked when he proposes a much more permanent solution—marriage!

"I wish only to kiss my wife," Cenzo growled. "On this, the first
day of the rest of our life together."

"You don't want to kiss me." She threw the words at him, and
he thought the way she trembled now was her temper taking hold.
"You want to start what you think will be my downward spiral,
until all I can do is fling myself prostrate before you and cringe
about at your feet. Guess what? I would rather die."

"Let us test that theory," he suggested and kissed her.

And this time, it had nothing at all to do with punishment.
Though it was no less a claiming.

This time, it was a seduction.

Pleasure and dark promise.

He took her face in his hands, and he tasted her as he'd wanted
at last. He teased her lips until she sighed, melting against him, and
opened to let him in.

He kissed her and he kissed her, until all that fury, all that need,
hummed there between them. He kissed her, losing himself in the
sheer wonder of her taste and the way that sweet-sea scent of hers
teased at him, as if she was bewitching him despite his best efforts
to seize control.

Cenzo kissed her like a man drowning, and she met each thrust of his tongue, then moved closer as if she was as greedy as he was.

As if she knew how much he wanted her and wanted him, too, with that very same intensity.

And there were so many things he wanted to do with her. But kissing her felt like a gift, like sheer magic, and for once in his life, Cenzo lost track of his own ulterior motives. His own grand plan.

There was only her taste. Her heat.

Her hair, which he gripped with his hands, and the way she pressed against him.

There was only Josselyn. His wife.

He kissed her again and again, and then he shifted, meaning to lift her in his arms—

But she pushed away from him, enough to brace herself against his chest. He found his hands on her upper arms.

"I agreed to marry you," she panted out at him, her lips faintly swollen and her brown eyes wild. "I refuse to be a pawn in your game."

"You can be any piece on the board that you like," he replied, trying to gather himself. "But it will still be my board, Josselyn."

He let her go, lifting up his hands theatrically. "By all means, little wife. Run and hide if that makes you feel more powerful."

He kept his hands in the air, his mock surrender, and laughed at her as he stepped back.

Because he'd forgotten, entirely, that they stood on those narrow stairs.

It was his own mocking laughter that stayed with him as he fell, a seeming slow-motion slide backward when his foot encountered only air. He saw her face as the world fell out from beneath him.

Don't miss
The Sicilian's Forgotten Wife
available September 2021 wherever
Harlequin Presents books and ebooks are sold.

Harlequin.com

Southern Sisters Mysteries by
Anne George
from Avon Books

MURDER ON A GIRLS' NIGHT OUT
MURDER ON A BAD HAIR DAY
MURDER RUNS IN THE FAMILY
MURDER MAKES WAVES
MURDER GETS A LIFE
MURDER SHOOTS THE BULL
MURDER CARRIES A TORCH
MURDER BOOGIES WITH ELVIS

And

THIS ONE AND MAGIC LIFE